Un-ruined

Un-ruined

a novel

Roger Vaillancourt

Un-ruined is a work of fiction. ©2022 Roger Vaillancourt. All rights belong to the author. Fair use quotations for review or scholarly purposes are welcome.

Published December 2022 by Malarkey Books

Cover art by Fred Free

ISBN: 9781088055441

malarkeybooks.com

To Nathan and Nick, who taught me how little I knew,
To Alex who gave me the room to see this through,
and to all the children of all the parents who don't know until they do.

1

I did look like him. Not like-a-twin similar, but certainly like-a-brother similar. That was what caught my eye when I saw the ad. Not because I was looking for an acting gig, and hell, I didn't even know what an "immersive acting experience" would be. But I needed work, and it said I should look like the picture. So I called.

The woman was named Marissa. As she described it, it made sense. I myself couldn't remember anything earlier than four. My earliest memory is pulling myself up to look out of the car by leaning on the window crank in my parents' Rambler. They got rid of that car when I was about five, so I guess my earliest memories were from my fourth year. Gramps died when I was three, and I don't remember him. So my experience confirms what she told me. Memory begins at four. Her son would be two next Tuesday. The contract was for a minimum of two years, with options out to four. Two years of guaranteed employment for showing up and playing house, in the role of her dead husband. It was a lot of money. No fool, I provided all the background materials and references, and when the contract arrived, I signed.

She sent me home with a book. Like two hundred pages printed out and held together with a binder clip. The story of how she'd met her husband, Neil, what he'd done for AON, their couple-hood in-jokes, their past residences, their relationships with their in-laws, their pet names (she called him "Bear"), their nickname for their unborn child, their plans for their old house in Vermont, the dead man's hobbies, the favorite toys and inclinations of the boy. The boy was named Calvert.

Later the same week, the videotapes arrived. I noted her husband's tics, his peculiar gesticulations and habits of moving, and imitated them all the time. Just did them. Much footage of him with the boy. That was useful. He seemed to be very physical; always hugging, tickling, tossing him into the air, on his shoulders, under his arm. He did a growl thing. I noticed it and then began to see it again and again. I couldn't make out what he was doing at first, but then finally in one clip she was walking with the camera and she walked up close as he tipped Calvert back in his arms and pressed close to the boy's ear and made the sound. It was a "rowr rowr rowr"-like chewing sound and the boy squealed like he was being tickled. But happy being tickled.

I came to the apartment when the boy was at daycare; Marissa took days out of work to do this. I learned the layout and the family routines. On weekdays I would be Dada from pre-dawn to 8 a.m., at which point I would leave and have the day to use as I wished. I would return at 6 p.m. each night to resume the role straight through to 8 a.m. Most of this time would be spent sleeping. Marissa and I would, for appearances' sake, share a bed. There was to be no physical intimacy of any degree, beyond what was needed in the presence of Calvert. Weekends were fully devoted to the role. Complete immersion, except for periodic "golf games," which would also be free time to use as I wished. I was much relieved to find out that I would not need to learn golf.

The day of the birthday was going to be when I first met the boy, or rather, it would be the day I *returned*. Marissa prepped me extensively the night before. In the darkened apartment, we leaned through the cone of light that shone down on the dining room table. There were flashcards with the faces and names of family members who would be present. They had all been briefed and would be prepared for me, or as prepared as their imaginations would allow. She quizzed me. She engaged in conversations with me. She threw my actual name in once or twice as a trial, but I was not shaken from character. After some hours, she seemed satisfied. She asked if I wanted to see the boy before tomorrow, not just in pictures, but the actual boy.

We padded to the door to his room, me avoiding the squeaky floorboard I'd learned of the week before. A tiny night light with a slowly spinning cover shone changing colors over Calvert. His sleeping eyes squinted in the shaft of light from the hall and he rolled over. I watched him for some time. He would be my son tomorrow. My mind sped through forged recollections of his birth, his infancy, his pre-verbal toddlerhood. I arrived at a counterfeit love. I stepped lightly in and kissed his head above his ear. He did not respond.

I returned to the hall and kissed Marissa lightly on the lips. She started back, shocked. She shook it off. Then she looked down, nodded, and without looking up waved her hand towards herself meaning "okay, one more time." She turned her face up and I kissed her exactly the same way again. She returned the kiss, and then stepped back and smiled at me beatifically.

"Okay. Started early. I'll see you tomorrow at Noon. Enjoy your last free night."

2

Birthday parties for young children are strange theater. Some of the children sense the formality of the event, and the obligation on them to have a good time within the invisible rules of what that means; they will only learn of a rule when they're being corrected for breaking it. This sometimes makes them anxious and fragile, particularly once they encounter the added components of gifts (for only one person) and sweets and goody bags and strange games. There's inevitably shouting and crying and it can be fraught. The parents have their own sets of anxieties: those putting on the party want everything to go well and for there to be peace and joy, as well as a positive impression on the guests. There may also be a desire to set the standard for what a great kid's party is, to model what a loving parent provides. The guests want their children to participate and yet not misbehave; nobody wants their kid to be the one who ruined the party. There's also the blind gamble of the gift: is it significant enough to warrant the invite to a party that had cost this much, yet not so great a gift that it is awkward to receive or appearing to strive towards showing off?

Knowing all this, I reminded myself that everyone at Calvert's party would be performing. It was awkward for everyone, and considering everything, I was probably better prepared than anyone else. I had an entrance to make. I would arrive after guests were present, after lunch, during playtime, but before cake and presents.

That morning I had used the dead man's brand of soap, and deodorant and shaving cream, I had laundered my clothes in the right brand of detergent, I had drunk tea instead of coffee. I had used spearmint gum instead of the peppermint that I'd preferred since I was a child. I was Calvert's dad, and my mind was firmly focused on my little boy whom I hadn't seen in many months. It was all about him.

As I walked in, Marissa was crouching down near Calvert and pointing back towards the doorway. Calvert swung his little head around, excited, and scrunched up his face for a second at me. I smiled, really broadly, confidently, truly happy to see his little face lit up, the first time I'd seen him awake in real life. I called to him "My little man!" just as I'd seen on the videos and he ran to me and I scooped him up and lifted him and did the rowr-rowr-rowr thing into his neck and he squealed and squeezed my neck in his little embrace and there was nothing forced or fake about it, for him or for me. It was a genuine moment of happiness for both of us, and I think the scent of the products and the fact that I was wearing a shirt that was his actual father's and which his mother had worn earlier in the same day could only help certify the reality of the moment. He didn't want to be put down for a while, and so I carried him on my hip and talked to him and walked over to Marissa and kissed her in a familiar way and then walked over to where Calvert was pointing, to the game the now-confused teenager at the gymnastics center had been organizing and running.

The other adults present fell neatly into two camps. First were those who didn't really know anything about Calvert's father, and were meeting him here for the first time today. They were relaxed and comfortable and polite. In the second group were those who had actually known Calvert's Dad; while they had been briefed on what was going to happen, they were each still coming to terms with it. The situation was clearly awkward for them, perhaps painful for some. Marissa and I were quite convincing, and Calvert was completely won from the moment I walked in, and this caused some people to be visibly uneasy. They wanted to go with it, to assist in the process, but were on some level horrified or repulsed. I suspect they may have felt pangs of mortality or perhaps it would be better called fungibility, horror-stricken to realize that with enough effort and intent, any person might be replaced with a talented likeness, and the world will spin along quite acceptably after this revision. I felt a swelling of professional pride while observing their responses, and the confidence it created made me more him.

Calvert didn't care. At some level he must have thought something was not quite right about me, but he didn't show it. Maybe his neurons were too busy growing, too busy with the work of gross motor skills and basic speech and object permanence to spare any bandwidth to assess parental authenticity. I suppose at some level a toddler lives in ongoing amazement, so why would anything register as off? His acceptance was joyous, and was what made it all work. He made it easier and easier as the day rotated. I only had to work hard to ignore one woman there. She was Calvert's aunt, either Marissa's sister or the dead man's sister, I didn't know. She paced and glistened and her hands moved restlessly and she looked unwell. I suspected she might be having a panic attack. At one point Marissa addressed her and the two of them went out to a lobby area, and Marissa returned alone.

She strode over to me, beaming brightly in a way that was self-protective, that was her only alternative to some expression that she wasn't going to allow here today, maybe one that would be scary to contemplate. She was powerful and disturbing and beautiful. Calvert did not reach out to her when she approached, and this made her smile a little bit more, as if this was now the only way she could go.

"Are you having a good time with Daddy after so long?" she asked the boy. "I'm glad, and I know Daddy's glad, too."

"Oh, yes I am," I said, meaning it.

3

It was called the cottage even though it had been built a century before as a family home. It was a house they had bought in Vermont before Calvert had been born. Theirs had been the invariant urban fantasy of having a place in the country, of owned real estate somewhere beyond NYC, with fantasies of children growing up with summers in the country and big family get-togethers in sunset lamplight and linen and pitchers of lemonade and games of horseshoes and maybe the dim, barely-acknowledged notion of retiring there to settle into their gray and slower ways together. The dream of the house had taken them through a process of learning that started when they saw the perfectional photo in the local real estate flyer on that holiday weekend he'd planned for them at the inn, cozy in their room with the hot tub, all the way through to the time in early October 2001 when, after her first month of widowhood, she remembered with a shock that the place existed, that the deeded land and structure was sitting there right off Rt 15 and now what the fuck? It was another of the things that had snuck up on her and sent her into a sharp jag of crying as if it were another death just heard about. That the cottage was still up there and what now to do with the remnants of the fantasies?

She had decided to keep it.

Part of the reason was because she felt she owed it to Neil, to the dreams he'd expressed of Calvert being there, of a little boy chasing clattering summer locusts and floating on a truck inner tube with warm air-dried skin facing the sky and cool damp skin facing the water within the ring of the black rubber, and exploring the forests behind the house pushing back away from the highway with a long walking stick as a pretend rifle and maybe, though she hated the idea of it, he liked to imagine the boy growing up with some locally appropriate skills like fly-fishing or deer hunting.

That he would be a boy of the city, who rode the subways himself and knew how to read the signs of an early-morning alley but be also a boy of the country, who could get his loved ones out of danger when the weather came in quickly or know just what to do when a youngster had wandered off from the family hike. Marissa felt an obligation to these dreams for Calvert. Even though they weren't her dreams, even though some of them were dreams she hoped would not happen, they were a representation of Calvert's father, and what was more important than keeping the weak spark of these dreams alive, or at least protecting them from indifference? Wasn't that what it meant to honor a loved one? Weren't we each just a compilation of our aspirations and hopes, and these surviving beyond the death of the body the most important goal for a loved one to continue?

Another reason she had decided to keep it was because it had been her and Neil's together in a way that nothing else was. After Calvert, the cottage was the only concrete thing in the world that they alone shared. There were parts of her husband built into the structure, the floor he'd installed alone while she stayed back in the city working through the weekend on an office project. The re-insulation that he had done at the high cost of a week of chronic, maddening itchiness in his limbs. And most of all the tile work they had figured out how to do together, and had installed with tiny little flaws that only they could see, flaws that they had created in their process of learning it and how they had talked about it being their own wabi-sabi, how it captured their moment in its imperfection and how she had loved that idea, what a minor miracle it was to be able to turn flaws that she would have normally obsessed about, felt regret about, and flip them to the other side entirely and make them a beloved thing. That had been a lesson to her, it informed how she thought about the world, and even in other areas of her life, when she would begin to feel the regret of a thing not perfectly done begin to come up in her, she would remember the tile work behind the tub, and remember herself and Neil in the warm water after a day of long work looking at the tiles and how the wabi-sabi was a thing to respect and adore. No, she was not going to sell the house, there was all their couple-hood built into it, into the work they'd done and all the joy of what, she knew but was not quite ready to admit to full consciousness, may have been the happiest days of her life, now behind her.

4

I have always been enraptured by the kitchens and bathrooms and living places of my new loves. It goes unnoticed in the noise of being in love, but there's a special joy in discovering for the first time the rooms in which your new love lives. Their most mundane spaces are imbued with a certain magic that this is where *they* toast the bagel or draw the bath or dry their hair, somehow the love you feel for the person can be felt in traces throughout their home. When I was a teen, it was her room in her parents' house, and when I was older, it was the woman's tiny apartment or her family's summer place. I loved her more by seeing her place, the mundane humanness of it, the un-swept crumbs on the otherwise-clean counter, the wear pattern on the doormat, the coils of the hair dryer cord turned in the same direction every morning winding tighter every day until she'd finally hang it by the plug and let it spin back to straight before picking it up and turning it in the same way as always, restarting the cycle. Her place was full of the soft marks she left on the world by being in it, and visiting it made me flush with a joy of commonwealth, that all objects present here had been blessed with her touch and presence as I felt myself blessed right then.

Marissa and Calvert's apartment had this for me after the birthday party. The party established me as the returned beloved and as the trusted employee both at once, and here in the apartment there was no extended family or friends from the prior life to test me. Only the boy and his mother, both with whom my ease was open. I rediscovered the persona I was playing, deepened it. I scanned the books on the shelf, the CD cases in the racks, the odd trinkets left in his desk drawer—the things too small to display but too important to throw away. I expanded my acquaintance with my character and did not judge him for his choices—my choices—but embraced them and found a place for them in myself. I had never liked Bruce Springsteen at all, but clearly Neil had. There were all the CDs, yes, but more so the little clutch of books about "The Boss" on the end of one shelf, the handful of issues of "Backstreets" magazine. I shook loose my memories of dislike and allowed room for new ones to re-form in the void created. This seemed like the right thing to do, to give up some of what I had been before in order to better be the man who was Calvert's father. It wasn't just professionalism, not just about earning the money, but about being as close to sincere as I could be for the boy. Somehow a little self-sacrifice was necessary and appropriate to the role and I did not begrudge it.

I found the pipe in the drawer of the entry hall, a fine-polished cherry wood pipe with bakelite stem, and lifted it to my nose to breathe in the resinous dark stamp of scented tobaccos and ash and damp and dust. It smelled like a tomb in a cathedral. That night I brought it to Marissa, asked her "Did Neil use this often?" and she saw the pipe and laughed, surprised, but slipped straight into a sudden sob and a shouted cry as if I'd pushed the pipe into her face like a gangster in a movie, cruelly.

After a moment she said, "No, not often. He was a little obsessed with it when he first got it. Like a week or so when he was all about it, but after that he used it only once in a while. He said it was a 'walking thing,' he'd do it when he was going to head out for a stroll. Oh, Jesus."

"Did Calvert see him use it?"

Marissa sighs. "Yeah, he did. The walks were usually the two of them. I think Neil liked being the Dad at the park with the pipe."

"Where's the tobacco?" There was none in the hall drawer, nor matches.

"I don't know, a coat pocket?"

She got up and headed towards the hall. Her own coat had been at the edge of the door, and she pushed it to the middle, opening the deeper end of the closet. There was no light bulb in it. She leaned into the dark opening, eclipsed by the door frame, consumed. From the position of the back of her head, I could tell that she was looking straight ahead, looking at nothing, working entirely by feel as she identified each coat by fabric and button or zipper, and reached into the pockets she was imagining in her mind, the pockets edged with fray or with crust or rip. Outside hand warmer pockets and inside breast pockets. She found things that were not tobacco, things she had to turn over in her hands and identify before replacing them and moving on. This inventory in the dark continued for some time.

At one point I thought I could hear her breathing in deeply, either to take in a smell or to push back an emotion or to offset a rising claustrophobia. She brought out her hand with an object in it, a small leather pouch. As it came to the light, it jingled, and in that moment we both knew it wasn't tobacco, it was small change. By the time it arrived out in the light she had no reason to be holding it, but seemed unable to put it back. She was frozen there with it in her hand. Then slowly, very deliberately, she turned and handed it to me.

"Here."

I remembered then that Dads jingle when they run, and need coins for gumball machines and other things. Dads pull out coins and hand them to their children for all kinds of reasons and situations. I took the coin purse and put it in my pocket. She returned to searching, but never found any tobacco.

Later that night I went to a smoke shop and asked the counterman to help me identify the tobacco that had been used in the pipe. He smelled the pipe as I had done and proclaimed "Dunhill Nightcap. But it's very stale, is this an estate pipe? It hasn't been smoked in a very long time, or if it has, it couldn't have been good."

I shrugged inarticulately. He resumed

"It's gotten moist, a little mildewed. You should probably ream it, use all of these" as he placed a box of pipe cleaners on the counter "with grain alcohol—not rubbing, but drinking—until it runs clean and then give the bowl a soak overnight with salt and alcohol to clear out the ghosts."

"Ghosts?"

"The ghosts, the old flavors. The old tobaccos leave their aromas behind and they can taint a fresh bowl. You want them gone. Clear out the ghosts. Salt and alcohol."

5

The little games are the best. Mammals learn through play, and small children are pure mammal, living close to the teat and thriving on the simplest play. Hide-and-seek and the unexpected bounce of the rubber ball and the silly dance and the tumbling block tower. These are the greatest joys and the most important work. For a small child, it is lonely work unless the adults around them notch back their own understanding and join them in the simple play. The adult needs to unwind all the life experience and all the layered subtlety and jadedness and remember how funny it is when the ball bounces wall to wall in the hallway and makes that funny sound. It's laugh-out-loud funny, and it's a wonderful thing to share and the joy of sharing that is what the child needs. He does not need educational games or letter-recognition drills or teaching tools. He needs simplicity and interaction and discovery.

And everything is to be discovered. It is all new, nearly every bit of it, and what is not new is comforting. It is a world we all came up through if we were lucky, and one we are lucky to have a chance to go back to with a small child. And I was being paid to do this with Calvert, to observe and share in the simplest moments and the simplest games as if they were happening for the first time ever, and to be the face he looks at then for a reaction and to be the one who smiles genuinely and says "Ha! Isn't that funny!" and in doing so, gives him the comfort and permission to smile and laugh himself.

I did a lot of this with Calvert, and I don't know if it was different from what Neil would have done. I'm not sure it's possible to know that; a child is a river, different every time you interact with him than he was before. Neil never knew this Calvert as I never knew the Calvert he held and loved, the one that struggled to form its lips and tongue into the shapes Neil made at him. That was Neil's shift, this is my shift. And if, instead of dying, Neil had been laid off from his job, or been caught in an affair, or been in a car accident that broke his pelvis, then he would have become a very different man and the nature of his relationship with Calvert would have changed, perhaps more than it has changed by his dying and being replaced by me.

But this was not the way it would be with Marissa. Or maybe it would. When she saw me, I'm sure I was to her some combination of employee and fellow play-actor, and the difference between me and Neil was vast and insurmountable and desirable in how it protected her husband's memory. But at night it would sometimes dissolve. We out of necessity slept in the same bed because Calvert was soon going to be going from the crib to a big-boy bed and that would begin the period of night-time visits, when he'd be letting himself into our room, and it was important to Marissa, critically important, that Calvert not find his parents in separate beds, or Mommy in the bed and Daddy on the chaise, like some permanent state of doghouse. It needed to be a happy couple there in the room, and happy was not about sex, but about togetherness and companionship, and for this reason we had to sleep in the same bed.

This made much sense, and was understandable, and she and I both stayed close to this understanding and we slept chastely on our far sides in little separate pools of mutual respect. But time passes, and after many nights, and after many long days, we found that in the night it was still two adults in a shared bed. It seemed fair and inevitable that one night she would shift over and lay her head on my chest and I would, without thinking, stroke her hair. It was hard work to live this performance for Calvert, and nobody else could know how hard it was; to comfort each other was appropriate and real. And so in a very different way from the play with Calvert, the situation in the parents' bed was still a reduction to simple terms, to basic instinct and sensation and, of a sort, familial love.

6

Days "at work" were surprisingly difficult.

At first it was relief, it was release back into my own true life, and it was the time when I would take care of both necessities as well as pleasures. This was where I'd go back to my own bed and nap in it just because I could, where I'd be greeted by the stale version of my own smell, re-encounter myself as partially foreign. On separate occasions I met a couple of friends for lunch, painting over each of their faces with the same puzzled expression as I described the work, described the boy and the woman and my role.

I would go back to my quiet apartment and pay my separate bills, my real bills, and do the small things that made the place feel still lived in; run the water in the sink until the red rust from standing ran away to clear; cleaned out the fridge in progressively more thorough steps, first the leftovers, then the items that had been bought new but never eaten, and then finally almost all of it as even the mustards and salsas had outlived their codes. By the end there was only a lonely quartet of an original six-pack lingering in the sallow light along with some butter cowering in its little transparent garage on the refrigerator door. In the earlier days I imagined that this was what it was like to be a consultant who worked out of town at a customer location for weeks. Home was a place I used to live, didn't live in now, but would someday live in the future.

But then one morning I stopped going.

Somehow that morning it had seemed like a silly thing to do, to visit that apartment. It felt indulgent and nostalgic, like I was going to check out an old bachelor pad. There were more pressing things to address, things that felt more important, things that I would have somehow found time to do in the midst of or at the end of my busy day in the office. A bottle of that Rioja that Marissa liked so much. Tickets for the children's concert that weekend. A new jacket, something with a finer cut that looked more the role. Reading Neil's calendar from the year before he died.

That last was an interesting exercise, a spiraling investigation. I started it almost on a whim, after I found it in his file drawer. His old dayplanner calendar. Why not, I thought, get a feel for what he'd been doing, how he'd been spending his time.

It must have been a private calendar, a personal one as opposed to some work-based calendar. Because there were a few work-related items on it, but they were the ones that intersected with the family life: out-of-town trips, weekend release meetings, company events in the evening. The rest of it was anniversaries and personal appointments and, in the last quarter of the year, dreams that were never to be realized. The end of December was two weeks blocked off with broad lines across both weeks and one word in block print in the middle: "COTTAGE."

That night we talked about it while Calvert threw his tiny parcels of pre-cut dinner on the floor in between stuffing fistfuls in his mouth.

"I'm gonna assume that vacation at the end of the year up at the cottage didn't happen."

"What vacation?"

"In his day-planner, it had the last two weeks of the year blocked off with 'COTTAGE' written across it. I assumed it was to spend the holidays there."

"Oh. Yeah, no, it didn't happen. We haven't been to the cottage."

"At all?"

"Not once. I'd told the local caretaker to rent it out as much as he can, to let it get use and keep it paid for. He manages that."

"Are we keeping it? The cottage?"

Marissa then looked at me for a long time without answering. Several expressions crossed her face. She looked very angry for a moment, and then she looked a couple of other ways momentarily, and finally she took a breath and released it slowly.

"Yes, Bear, we'll be keeping it."

7

The lot next to the house in Vermont had been turned years back and sown with Kentucky bluegrass, but there's still a lot of hay mixed in there, which must be from back in the day when it was briefly a paddock. The last owners had been in the house for generations, and the last generation, the original grandchildren, had been undone by their good fortune. They had come into a bunch of money on a lottery ticket, and bought two horses and fitted out the property for them. But they were new to money and they calculated poorly, managed the small remainder of the winnings indiscriminately, and within five years they found themselves deeply poor, house-poor and horse-poor.

The horses went first, achingly loaded into a stranger's trailer while the two children cried and wailed and the parents pretended to wipe their sweaty brows while dabbing their own eyes. The couple didn't last long after that; Dad found a girlfriend up in Burlington, and Mom and the girls headed down to Pennsylvania and into a row house with her parents. At first the realtor had a notion of trying to sell it as a gentleman's horse farm, but that was never going to work, it had gone into a sad state already, paddock fencing rotting and dropped by the posts that sensed their shift ending, the roof fishmouthing and the yard returning to native wild growth. Fixing up the paddock and the little barn would have taken a big investment, and would have solidified it as a niche property, so they brought in the end-loader and took it all down in a day and trucked it out before tilling the yard and spray-seeding on the bluegrass blend. It would do better as an "authentic" local property ready for some young couple looking for a country place to make up to their own vision. And so it was when Neil and Marissa had first seen it.

The bulb-tipped grass from the hay still springs up through the broader-leafed lawn, subtly at first. It's just a weed you think, looking at it, it's just a bit of something blown in or dropped in a sparrow's shit, but then up it continues, it arcs up impressively over the stubby lawn with a firework's trajectory, making the lawn below it look a little sorry, a little too regular and orderly and compliant, all the little blades stopping just at the same height and bunching up in anonymous safety and fear. And this tall sprig of oatgrass is never far from the next sprig of oatgrass, usually just more than its own height away from the next one flinging itself above the deep green blades of foreign nonsense, and beyond that sprig flies the next one and then the next one again.

Neil had not seen them this way, he had always thought of the lawn as a thing that could be done well or poorly, and consistency and lushness was the signature of success, and he plucked the hay sprigs carefully before he mowed, gently turning the thing from where it emerged from the dirt, to turn the root or as much of the root as he could to loosen it, and then pulled it out whole and tossed it into the cloth newsboy paper sack slung across his shoulder so that it would not be chopped and sown back into the lawn when he mowed. His technique was methodical and effective, and the hay came out slowly that summer, every week plucked like some gold from a seam, into the bag and then into the compost with the coffee grounds and eggshells and farm share they could never finish every week, to be converted by the night crawlers to fine soil for the potted pansies in the window boxes. But he could never truly get ahead of it, the hay was there sown so broadly and so deeply in the kernels that waited over each winter; some that sprouted but could not work through the lawn's thatch and died there, some that were pushed back down by the roots and were cycled in that slow dark surf up and down pushed by rains and frost heaves until the time was right, until Neil was gone and they could feel the sun and could sense the break in the thatch and it was time now for this one to push up and out and through the morning air into the sky, rocketing at the sun.

8

Calvert's best friend at this time was a little girl named Samantha. They had met at the "Gymnasticks" class, a wholesome combination of jumping, tumbling, and taiko drumming, where both of them displayed particular affinity for not doing what was expected. The pair of them were scofflaws, preferring to get apart from the group and flirt with one another in toddler ways, like parallel play and by following and surprising one another. They encouraged each other. They were fortunate in that their parents were amused by it, and considered it healthy and appropriate and allowed it. Samantha's mother was Jessica; the first impression I had of her was kindness. It seemed a remarkable quality in this scene, among the young-affluent-parent set, which as a group seemed very prone to anxiety and competitiveness and false confidence and judgment. Maybe this was due to the general selection criteria for young affluence, which favors the confident and aggressive, yet still fused to the guideless task of child-rearing, which instills in everyone at some level the sense that they are parenting incorrectly or incompletely or inexpertly, which makes the fall back to false confidence and easy judgment even more common.

True kindness in these adults was a bit of a rarity, but Jessica gave it freely to her children and to the adults around her, and it made her seem supernatural. Her calmness enrobed her like the clouds and linen around Christ in a painting, and there were times I would find myself trying to silently will her to hold her fingers in that way, with the index and the middle extended but held together, so that as her peaceful smile shone on her face, she would fully look the part, ready to extend a blessing, to exhort the yoga-pants- or biking-shorts-clad parents in fraught competition around her to feel the benign negligent love of the universe upon them and to admit their own faults and fears and own them and be peaceful in their flaws with their children. But she never did deign to bless or exhort them, because that would have been presumptuous, that would have been superior, that would have been not like her to do, though I wished she would do it.

No, for all this I didn't fall in love with Jessica, and there are reasons why not. First, I am a professional, and my role was beloved husband and father, and my choices were first and foremost Neil's choices, and so it could not even be considered. Second, Jessica was not available for it, her peace and joy were firmly placed in the life she was engaged in, she didn't have the cracks into which an infidelity needs to set its tiny wedge. Finally, it would have just been ugly, and while not a classically beautiful woman, she had a glory to her that infidelity would have ruined like a creeping mold. So leave it be now that while Jessica was a rare creature in the place where we all resided, it was not her that would engage my love and devotion. It was the relationship between Calvert and Samantha that would do this.

Calvert and Samantha gave back to the world the attitudes that the world had given them. They were open to others and assumed goodness in them, they were open to new things and to learning, they were open to play though the rules may not be clear or even extant. They were sweet children, as inclined to grouchiness or tantrum as any in their times of woe, but generally smiling and playful and happy. They did not look overly to their parents to guide their actions, they did not decide their next move based on whether it would be corrected or praised, they knew they had wide latitude, and that there was delight available in the trying of things. They were not attracted to the bullies or the scrappers, they were not interested in winning the affections of any of their classmates over another, they were unmoved by these things. This made them stand out a little from the other children in a similar way to how Jessica and I stood out a bit from the other parents. Misfits happy to be so. This attracted them quickly to one another. They interacted with the other children, tried out tiny friendships with them, but none of those seemed to stick. It was sad and a little painful to watch some of those interactions, to see the sweet openness met with tiny dominations or minute brutalities. It made my heart ache a little, it was hard to not rush in to counter the insult to rightness. But I did not rush in, nor did Jessica, we had faith that our children would steer themselves away from these morbidities, and they did. So it was not a long time before they found each other and that was a thing that seemed to stick.

At the Gymnasticks class Jessica and I ended up talking because we saw this happening, saw the kids clicking differently from the larger group, and so we chatted each other up on the second or third class and were pleased to note that this person we were speaking to seemed reasonable and pleasant. There were feints in conversation we each seemed to use to ensure this, little tricks like alluding neutrally to habits or positions we actually hated (ugh, day-trading) and seeing how the other reacted, or dropping obscure references to things that were not broadly popular at that time, but which indicated a certain affinity (obscure Five Points historical trivia). We passed each other's tests. One of my tests was Marissa's: determining if Jessica had ever smoked, or even tried smoking. Marissa was of the mind that people who smoked but quit early, or better yet, tried briefly but for whom it never clicked, were much more to be trusted than people who had never tried it at all. There was a need for proof of engagement in life experience and self-learning, and smoking was a solid metric. A person who has never tried betrayed a lack of life experience and a person who has never quit betrayed a lack of self-learning. Jessica fessed to smoking sporadically during her sophomore and junior years of college, even to meeting a boyfriend on a smoke break. The smoking outlasted the boyfriend, but not by much. This was a good score on this scale.

The first playdate was scheduled for Samantha's house at the end of that same week.

There we all discovered that the two kids were mad for drawing, coloring, with sideline interests in dinosaurs and other animals. Their drawings were not really representative yet, they would have occasional flashes of recognizability, but we proud parents projected our interpretations onto their work, to see in their scribblings the things they said were drawn there. We received these illuminations of their works like visitations from a god, shocked, obvious once they pointed them out, "of course!", yes, there's the tiger, in the corner, his stripes, of course; though there was no outline of a tiger, no framing that an adult would use, no tooth or claw or feline crouch, there were inarguably stripes there, crouched, ready to pounce, of course yes now I see the tiger.

Jessica offered coffee or tea and introduced me to her husband by way of a photo of the two of them before Samantha had been born, them happy, somewhat formal as a stranger took their photo with a camera just handed to him, in some picturesque crumbling old-world location, probably Italy I assumed. Her husband's name was Jeffrey. I knew then that I would call them J&J when I talked about them to Marissa, perhaps we would "go over to J&J's" for dinner one night, or "have J&J over," suddenly they were visible as embedded components of our life. But it wasn't about them.

We mostly watched Calvert and Samantha play. Even from before the first playdate, Calvert and Samantha would enjoy little reveries in the presence of the other, and observing these was a pleasant agony. The sweetness of it was something I could feel physically. Samantha would be talking, babbling about her picture while she was deep in the drawing of it, and Calvert would stop what he was doing and just watch her and listen to her and seem to emit raw affection from his tiny pores. Basking in her presence. She would do the same at other times when he was on a roll, she would be still and smile looking at him as if in possession of some delightful secret that only the two of them knew, and sometimes these reveries would accelerate physically into little expressions of excitement, like bouncing on their toes, or suddenly sprinting to the other side of him, or most touchingly, in the form of a tiny arm that went out around the shoulder of the other. They each did this regularly, would come up to the other one, and touch them gently, absentmindedly, lovingly. An arm around the shoulder, or a pat of the head, or a nudge of the elbow, or the knocking of a knee with a knee. They each did it. They also were keen to give each other things, to hand each other markers or goldfish crackers or toys or anything. They gave freely to each other, and in equal proportion each to the other.

It was magical to observe, because it was so natural to them. They had not been taught to do this, nor particularly encouraged to focus on this other little person by any parent or other external force. They had just found one another, and these interactions sprang from them alone. It was a pure, natural expression of love. Jessica saw it too, I watched her see it, and once or twice after something particularly sweet passed between our two children, I would look to her and she to me and we would smile at each other in the shared joy of it. It was so sweet and innocent and lovely and most of all rare. The rarity of it was what struck me most, what made me so protective of it. It was like seeing the last pair of an extinct breed, there in front of you, and the urge to protect them from the world, from change, from their own future, was overwhelming.

There was also, truth be told, the tiniest bit of jealousy. It occurred to me that Marissa and I could have between us something distantly related to this, something unsullied by sex or jealousy, but it wasn't the same, ours had a commerce at its heart that made it hopelessly adult even without the other adult components. She and I also did not have the raw attraction that Calvert and Samantha had. That was what I was most jealous of. The acceptance each had of the other, that the other one was perfect as-is. Neither had any designs to change the other, there were no dreams of improvement or refinement; they were content with what was there before them now. This was a thing to be aspired to, a thing to be deeply, shamefully jealous of. The protective impulse was selfish, was next-level jealousy; I wanted nobody else beyond Jessica and myself to have access to it, to be deigned to observe it, to have the privilege of enjoying it vicariously. It was too precious a commodity, too fragile and enviable for the world to know even of its existence.

I don't think Marissa ever really saw it for a long time. The Gymnasticks class was my thing with Calvert, and she was happy for it to be ours alone, and so by extension the friendship with Jessica was mostly mine to manage, and the relationship between Calvert and Samantha was not something she had regular access to. She certainly knew that they were friends, I made it clear that Calvert had clicked with Samantha, and that theirs was a friendship that should be encouraged and facilitated, and over time she was witness to a playdate or two and saw some of their interactions, at least enough to know that Samantha would be his friend for a time and that this was a good thing.

I felt the pain of it ending even while I watched them hold each the other's tiny hand, them not knowing, not knowing at all that things would change.

9

I thought that Marissa had the date wrong at first. I thought she'd come to me a year early with her earnest face to ask if I would be re-upping. She caught me as Calvert and I were returning from a walk around the block on a May Saturday, I still had a smoking ember of tobacco caught in the groove of my running shoe after knocking out the pipe against my heel out on the sidewalk. I put Calvert down and stooped to pick the smoking tobacco strand out of my shoe, it blowing half sweet tobacco smell, half burning rubber smell, as the boy ran off to his room and Marissa said "Here, I need to talk to you," and she picked up my hand and walked me towards the dining room. I carried the strand between my thumb and index finger, it smoldering like an incense stick, not wanting to drop it on the rugs or the hardwoods.

She opened the discussion in a surprisingly formal and corporate way, it was clear she was falling back into some habits of work. She started by saying something about how well it had been working the past two years and how she'd undertaken the whole thing in a spirit of cautious optimism, but her thoughts tumbled on as she described how she was really very pleasantly surprised at how wonderfully it had come together, how really healthy it seemed to be for Calvert, who was now almost four, and how I had taken the work so seriously and so much to heart. I smiled, I could feel myself smiling. I was pleased with my work and did it with deliberation and care, and it made me quite proud that she appreciated it and that she thought it was as good for Calvert as it seemed to me this was. Really she was making me feel quite happy. Then she pivoted.

"So with things moving this well, and where we are, we have two options; we kill you off now, or by the end of the month; or we go for another two years understanding that you'd have to keep the pace at least at par. I know what I'd prefer, but I want to hear your thoughts first."

It's an odd thing to hear your own demise presented as an equal option to things continuing the same. As if there may be insufficient criteria by which to pick, as if it were a question of vanilla or chocolate. I suppose it always is this kind of a choice, but it never gets thought of that way. It's either a really shitty alternative to what the person pointing the gun at you wants you to do, or it's an apparently simpler option than a horribly complex and painful life for the suicidal. But rarely is it a "side salad or baked potato" kind of toss-up. Yet this is how it sounded to me.

"I'm not going anywhere if you'll still have me," I said, barely thinking before I answered. My answer was sincere and uncluttered by any selfishness for my prior life or fatigue of this one. I felt at home here now, I loved Calvert genuinely, and I loved Marissa in a familial, nonsexual way, and I had no desire to leave. This was my beautiful house and this was my beautiful wife and Calvert was my beautiful boy and even though it was in some ways all fake and all a lie, it was far more real than all the other lives I had once imagined for myself, or could imagine for myself now, and to leave it now would be to step from a warm, lush greenhouse out into a cold, barren steppe.

Marissa smiled broadly and said "Oh, good, I'd hoped you'd say that. I'm really glad." She put her hand over mine on the table and squeezed it tightly. She then took three of the sheets on the table and stacked them and tore them up quickly, tearing again and again until the pieces were the size of postage stamps. Stamps of a country I would visit someday. She took the remaining two sheets and turned them to me and said, "Just a couple of places to initial, and then one to sign, and we're all set. This is great."

It occurred to me then that traditionally a review is when pay increases are discussed, and that we didn't talk about it. I mean, in some ways it seemed too crass to discuss, but this was an employment discussion and we had just both agreed that I'd done a great job and we wanted me to continue, so wouldn't it be the time . . . ?

"Any adjustment in compensation?" I asked, quietly, as I read the renewal contract. I did not look up as I asked this, but Marissa was very quiet for a time and I imagined her expression had probably darkened a bit.

When I looked up she was looking directly at me, expressionless. The excitement had drained from her. She said, very neutrally, "What do you want?"

"I don't know, I guess I just realized that this would be the time to talk about it."

"Do you want a bonus?" she asked with a little edge. "Do you want a four percent increase to keep aligned to the standard of living, since you have all those . . ." She stopped herself just as her tone was ramping up. She looked away to the corner of the table, then back at me. Hurriedly, insincerely, she continued.

"What can I do to show my appreciation for what you are doing every day for Calvert?"

Then she stopped speaking, silent, charged in coiled wait.

Now it is true that I didn't need more money. I had no significant expenses to cover apart from the rent on my old place, which by this time I was subletting. But I was creating this uncomfortable interaction for some reason, in the service of some desire I hadn't fully figured out myself. I was hoping for something, some sort of expansion of the embrace. Something that demonstrated additional legitimacy. I seemed to be asking to be more Neil. I wanted an increase in my Neil-ness.

"How about use of the car?"

The family had a nice Mercedes CL that had to be washed every time it was taken out because of the dust it accumulated from lack of use. We had all driven together in it two or three times, for specific outings beyond the city. I wondered about the dust, how there got to be so much of it inside a weather-protected Manhattan parking garage. Somehow in my mind without really thinking, I came to realize that it was the dust from truck brakes and car tires and pulverized concrete and atomized winter garbage and crushed pigeon bones and even abraded subway rails, all of it swept in through the cracks of the walls and blown in and out as the cars were valeted front to back. The accretion of things being what they were, and where they were.

"For what? What do you intend to do with it?"

"Just to drive it on occasion. It's a nice car, and it's a shame to see it never used, and I'd like to go for a drive sometimes, just out of the city. I guess to be Calvert's Dad further out."

"Your license is current? Valid? Your real one?"

"It is."

"Do you have Neil's? What's that got on it before it needs to be renewed?"

I took Neil's wallet out of my pocket and opened it and slid out the license. It was valid through his birthday in 2007. Plenty of time, and even then I could renew by mail. The photo looked familiar, like I remembered myself from a couple of years ago in a mirror somewhere else, somewhere I could not quite recall.

"Good through 2007. You would want me to use this?"

"Would I want you to be Calvert's father and the co-owner of the car and the named party on the insurance card?"

"And your husband?" I added.

She ignored my comment. "Goes without saying, yes, you would be Neil when driving the car. Yes, you can have use of the car. Not entirely at random, we'll need to coordinate your use of it so I'm not left hanging."

"Thank you!" I said cheerily. Then I pushed it a bit. "But are you still mad at me?" I smiled in a manner I hoped would come across as naive and winning and couple-cute. She said my name, my birth name. She did not call me Bear.

"I'm not fond of secrets or surprises. I'm not happy that you sprung this on me like this. I'm relieved that your request is not a big thing, but I don't like the shtick. Let's not do this kind of thing again. I have a lot to manage with this whole situation, perhaps much more than you appreciate, and really the last thing I need is for you to be adding to the long list of things I need to try to anticipate and be ready to deal with. I need you to be on my side, to be working with me by looking ahead and thinking ahead. Okay?"

"Okay, sure," I said, serious.

"If you need a thing, if you want a thing, I need you to just have a conversation with me about it and not do it in a leveraged way. Haven't you found me reasonable to deal with?"

She stopped talking. The question wasn't rhetorical.

"Yes, yes. Of course." She stayed silent, she was waiting for more. "You've been nothing but reasonable and considerate. I'm sorry, that was a dumb idea. I just wasn't really thinking ahead, I guess I didn't prepare for this discussion. Actually, to be fair, you didn't really prepare me for this either. You kind of sprung this on me, and while that's not an excuse, I think it's fair to say we each could have done a better job on this. I mean, really."

This knocked her back a bit.

"Okay, yes. Yes, that's fair."

She was quiet for a moment, but from her face I knew more was coming.

"And if I'm honest about it, I probably didn't prepare you for this conversation because I didn't want you to think yourself out of it. But that's not fair to you. Sorry."

"Thanks. We both care a lot, I think. I think we are working together pretty well, really." I signed the sheet and initialed in the places where the highlighter had touched. I swiveled the document to her and handed her the pen. She signed quickly.

"Yes, it's true. And I was just . . ." She was still flustered and seemed to be trying to shake off an unpleasant idea.

"Marissa, can I ask you something?"

"Yes, of course."

"What were you going to say if I'd said no? Is that what you were thinking about?"

"Ugh. Yes. Do you want to talk about this now?"

"I kind of do. I think this might be the right time. Now that we know we're not changing anything, that anything we talk about is out somewhere in the future. It's hypothetical today."

"It's just estate planning."

"Yes exactly," I said, not really thinking, not really hearing the words, just eager to get to the next part of the conversation. Marissa seemed to settle in, she seemed to be preparing herself to recount a long, complex train of logic.

"So let's take a step back. The reason you're here is so that Calvert will have memories, positive memories of his father. Since Neil died when Cal was not even two, and the earliest memories most people can access are from around four years old, it made sense to do a two-year stint. It's worked out very well. I couldn't be happier, I wouldn't change a single detail.

"But Calvert's father dies. You're not replacing Neil, you're just delaying his extinction. As Cal gets older, it's going to be harder and harder to do this, to keep it going as Neil, and the point of it—the whole point—was to preserve Neil just a little bit longer. You aren't the song, you're the echo."

That stung a little bit, I have to admit.

"And the goal is not to prevent Calvert the pain of losing his father. It's to prevent him the much greater pain of never having known his father. Neil dies."

"Right, I get that. Neil dies. You don't have to keep saying it."

"You die, Bear. The person I'm interacting with here dies. You go back to who you were before you answered the ad. I go back to finish being a widow. Neil ceases to be."

"But I'm kind of more interested in hearing about the details, the logistics of how Neil actually dies."

"I can see why you'd be curious, but it's really academic to you. You won't be there for it. And you knowing the plan would only be a curse, don't you think? Like one of those stories where the person is told of his death by the fortuneteller and then he spends all his time trying to avoid it and then gets caught up in some ironic version of the death foretold?"

"But you've got a plan, you know what you're going to do."

"Bear, don't worry. It's all going to be fine, and it's not happening anytime soon, so please just try not to get hung up on it."

This was a mode for Marissa, "not going there." Against this mode, I could only circle her like a cat around an aquarium batting on the glass. There was nothing more coming, no more information available, there would be no progress or satisfaction. I comforted myself by thinking that she did this because she wanted somehow to "protect" me, then I distressed myself by thinking that she wanted or needed to prevent me from knowing something bad, something that would make me sweep up the sheets on the table and tear them and spit at her "fuck you, this is fucked up and I'm out."

But I would not know, so there would be two years more. I'm good on the short strokes, I can compartmentalize well. Okay, fine.

I stood up and held my arms out to her. She stood and we embraced. I said quietly just past her shoulder "I love that boy."

She said, "I know. That's why."

10

There is, up on the Merritt Parkway towards its northernmost end, a bridge that is decorated in the center of its span with a tall set of wings. I don't know whether they are intended to be inspiring or cheerful, but they always surprised me when I saw them, and I always found them intimidating. They seemed folded, they seemed to be standing in wait, and as I drove closer to them, I thought they might open, they might spread and flap like an annihilating angel in a movie, and then the end will be upon me and visible.

I drove past them, hiding in my feigned indifference, wearing the same face I used in school when I didn't want the teacher to call on me. The wings stood, unmoving, roosted on the abutment, and even in the rearview I saw them, tiny, hoping for nothing to change in their profile, and nothing did and they receded to a fine point, still the same, until they had reached the granularity of my vision and they had gone microscopic, down to the realm of bacteria and virus and small scary things all abstract but still very much there.

It was a "golfing" weekend away, so I had kissed my beautiful wife and my adorable child and left them, hefting the bag of clubs out and into the trunk where I'd leave them in the dark until I returned Sunday. I was actually going to the house in Vermont. I hadn't told Marissa this. It had not been hard to find the address in the file cabinet, it would be harder to get the damned MIO GPS to work, but fuck it, I thought, I can just buy a map somewhere off 91 in Brattleboro when I stop for lunch.

I negotiated access to the car because there are places in my mind that are only accessible by driving. A long road trip, one of greater than two hours of steady driving, settles my mind into a deep meditative state. I'm sure that if you put an EEG on me, you'd see interesting things on a long drive, a slow death of Beta settling into pure Alpha waves, the steady, conscious opening of the mind and the athletic streaming of thought to thought, a graceful scree run over broad, sharp riprap.

Deep green flowed along both sides of the highway. It was high summer and where in winter the view would be naked distant parallax shifts of cold-storage buildings and water towers, in summer it's a close-in velvet chute of weeds and vines and ivy and trees broken by rare deep drops down power-line corridors cut into the seething flesh.

There were ignored places there, too. There were strange abutments to the highway, where behind a house or commercial building there's a neglected fence and collapsing stone wall between it and the highway. There were small mysterious buildings, warts of infrastructure where communication lines met or water shut-offs hid. As I passed each of these, I visited them momentarily, I imagined the damp concrete always in the dark, the pumps or relays toiling there in unmolested quiet like monks over their codices. Then I flew back out into the sunlight and up to the crossbar of the high-tension tower, to narrow sudden vertigo and electric peril.

Further north, up into the Green mountains there were the runaway truck ramps, long arcing swimming pools of gravel. I was surprised how often I'd seen them with two deep grooves in them that told the story of a driver's fear and rising panic, of the hard decision to dive in while there's still time weighed against the painful delay and phone calls he'd need to make if he did, the hard money it would cost to get it pulled out and repaired versus the injury and death he might cause if he tried to ride it out. How for any driver that uses it, that ramp will be a place etched in his memory, that when he passes it again, it will be a place he really lived briefly, the location of bad time lit in flashing amber, of an illness that nearly but did not kill him.

There were the tracks of police cars off the highway, the special paths only they may drive. They were so tempting. Sometimes, on toll roads, these would run out to the right like abrupt VIP exit ramps, way too short and steep to drive comfortably; I'd have had to slam on the brakes and the front bodywork might scrape as the car climbed it. These ramps always had driver's-side keypads and rolling gates. Sometimes the gate was open, just sitting open. Even though the road it led to was probably some nowhere country lane, I felt a flutter of desire to take the exit. Because it's a closed thing that was just right then open. It was a diagram of opportunity. It was an adventure beckoning. I have never taken one. I know that if I did, the other drivers would assume mine was an unmarked vehicle, or that I was an off-duty officer. I would probably get away with it and then be on a random back road, still stuck in the car with my adrenaline crash and with my disappointment.

But those were the least interesting police car trails. The interesting ones ran across the median, and the ones that interested me most were not the straight cuts across where I could see the other side where I'd have to floor it in the passing lane to avoid getting rear-ended at 80, but the ones where the trail went off from the highway into the median and then went up to a short crest and into deeper woods and I could see no daylight from the other side. I knew that the trail must connect over to the other side of the highway, probably more directly than I imagined it did, but my mind preferred to think that there was a place in the median, there was a building or a campsite there that they stopped at, even just a bench or two where officers would stop and talk and smoke and sip their lukewarm coffees and listen to the traffic that runs along both sides, tucking them in snugly to their conversation.

This is what driving did for me, it made the world more than it actually is. It restored the mystery behind everything just out of reach, the mystery that was there when I was in the back seat and an adult was unspooling this road for me, when the book I was reading on the drive could click into perfect synch with landscape going by over there, when the movie I saw last night sleepy in the motel might be taking place just up that exit ramp, when the music on the radio describes the thoughts of the people walking way off in the distance beyond that fallow field.

The radio played old Roxy Music, "More Than This," and it was perfect to my thoughts. It wasn't sad, it wasn't despairing. It was joyful because the song was wrong, there was more than this, there is always more than the eye reveals, there are scales and scales beyond it, leaping increases of magnitude, each fully furnished with incident and detail and the real and the imagined are no different from here as they recede into the deep distance, nor should they be.

There was something heaped on the pavement at the edge of the median. I saw it from far off, and my brain cycled through ideas of what it might be. It was so shapeless that it must have been something from a truck, a beanbag chair or bag of clothes that flew out of the back of a pickup on the way to UVM.

Then no, it had forms that showed structure, it was broken furniture.

Then for a moment I felt a flicker of terror that it might be a person, someone just struck moments before by a trucker who didn't hear the sound or thought it was a tire de-treading.

Then it was closer, it was a deer. It was a deer.

I saw soft downy brown and white fur and the raw red flesh and the white of bone and darker soft maroons and purples and dull yellows strewn around. Stripes of white that were ribs, extending up into the air. The ribcage was open to the sky like a flower. It hurt me for a moment, inside my ribs I felt the breeze of the cars going by, my organs and guts cowered within me, not wanting that for themselves, hiding from knowing, pretending I hadn't seen it.

11

I was close to the cottage. But this last part was the most difficult.

The countryside depends upon recollection. It is poorly demarcated for the newcomer and sometimes only local knowledge tells you whose house is whose, why it is this way, what it even is. Directions are given relative to landmarks that existed in the past, but are gone now. House numbers rare, mailboxes can help, but they are often decapitated, useless even to themselves. Over there was a mailbox post of poured concrete, with scuffs along it where the bat was broken, probably wrists or an arm broken, too. The batter and the mailbox owner perhaps both known to the Nurse Practitioner who set the bones, the whole story obvious to her when his friends brought him to the urgent care in the car with the broken side-window. The whole story laid out there, transparent. The countryside is tiny, claustrophobic in its powers of recollection.

I had more than just the address I'd written down. I'd seen the house in the tiny black and white photo on the hallway bookshelf, so I knew the visual I was looking for, I knew the structure. The address used the local street name, but on maps this street appeared only as the state route number. The concrete mailbox was a neighbor two houses down. There it was, Marissa and Neil's little cottage. I turned the radio way down so I could think. I hadn't imagined the house being this color. It was a brownish/greenish/gray. In the photo I imagined the color to be something more classic, a blue/gray or even maybe red. But I saw that the color was an earth tone from a 1990s palette. It didn't look old-fashioned, it looked like an old fashion. The color was from a different time, and it didn't quite belong anymore.

The house was in good repair, though. The caretaker was doing his job. There didn't seem to be anybody there; I didn't see any cars on the property, and the house looked closed up, none of the sash windows were open, and it was hot enough that they would have been if somebody had been inside. I had a flicker of concern with how I would greet the caretaker if I should see him, who I would be. I wasn't sure whether Marissa had explained me to him, or whether he had ever met Neil. Since I had wanted to go into the house, and I had a key, I decided that I would be Neil.

The driveway was just two dirt tracks crushed through the grass, with a grass strip in between. It had grown high enough that I could hear the stalks falling under the car as I drove up. The radio whispered a song I couldn't quite recognize. I stopped the car and got out. It was very quiet, and the car ticked and I could hear insects in the field alongside and in the forest behind. I swiveled around and there, across the street and beyond a broad lawn, was the lake. I heard a distant boat, far up the lake, going somewhere at speed. I knew from the map that the lake is closed, there's no river access out. The boat was going fast, but nowhere.

The key was on the ring, on the same ring as the car key. They are Neil's keys. I rolled them in my hand in a familiar way, folded and unfolded them along the ring as I did before putting them in my pocket, first the flat keys against the bloated car key, then the other-way-round. Keys to important things, keys that define the scope of who I am. Up to the porch. The porch boards were painted, not stained. They'd been painted more recently than any other part of the house I could see. They were shiny and bright, but the patterns of paint showed where the boards were worn beneath, where this coat of new paint had gone over wood worn bare by feet, and places where the paint was solid layers deep, like tree rings. The screen door was old, old-style, wood with in-set screen panels and bowtie latches holding them in. I knew before I opened it how it would sound when I let it go and it slammed. It was that kind of screen door.

I opened the deadbolt and went in. The weather-sealing on the door gave way reluctantly. The place was cool, it smelled like a vacation house, it was not lived in daily, there were no food smells, it's pleasantly musty. It smelled like slow-floating dust baked in sunlight from the windows.

Behind me I heard a footfall and I turned and he was there. He must have been the caretaker. He was an older man, and he had one of those familiar faces, he looked like someone from somewhere before. His face was serious.

"What are you doing?"

Now I expected a caretaker to have a certain responsibility for security, to keep the place closed and unmolested, but I was taken aback by his approach. It was rather aggressive. From his tone, I assumed that he had never met Neil, that he only dealt with Marissa and so would never have expected to find a man here letting himself into the house.

"Oh, hey. No, I'm Marissa's husband. I'm Neil." I put out a hand to him.

He half-grabbed the front of my shirt and pushed me back with his closed fist, my back flat against the door, and growled "No you fucking aren't, you idiot. You don't even remember who I am, do you?"

Oh, wait. Yes, I did. His face wasn't familiar because "it's one of those faces"; it's familiar because I'd seen him before. He was a relative.

"I'm Calvert's Grandfather, stupid. The Grandfather of the little boy you're playacting being Daddy for, you fuck."

Oh shit, it was Neil's father.

Early on, Marissa had been clear about minimizing my interaction with Neil's parents. It made sense, I was sure they weren't fond of the whole idea, so whenever Calvert visited with them or came by it was when I wasn't around. It was planned carefully, and I had respected that. It seemed appropriate. I'd seen them at the initial birthday party, but not since. Ah fuck.

"What are you doing here?" he asked again.

"I just wanted to get familiar with the place before we were up here with Calvert. I needed to know it a little."

"And you took his car?" He pointed down off the porch with his chin.

"Marissa is fine with it, we discussed it."

"Oh so Marissa is fine with it, is she? She's fine with you doing some research before a summer vacation together, the little family making more sweet memories up at the cottage? Well, we'd better learn you right, then."

He got a fresh grip on my shirtfront and pulled me into the house. I left the keys dangling in the lock, and tried not to fall as he pulled me forward.

"Now this here is the living room, it's furnished from two places; some of these things Neil and Marissa bought at stores up here, and the rest of them—like that two-tiered end table and that wooden stool—were given to them by Neil's parents, because they were pieces of furniture from the house he grew up in and they meant something to him."

"See this low coffee table? We play cards on here, mostly Rummy 500. Neil learned that game from his grandmother, who could never resist picking up even a huge discard pile, because she always knew she could make something from it and it's better to have something than nothing. Even though the goal of the game is to have nothing. Neil picked up that habit, too, of taking big discard piles. Be sure to do that. Now, let's look at the kitchen."

I was dragged through the hallway to the kitchen, and I realized that there was probably a time when this man dragged Neil this same way as a teenager when Neil had done something stupid or dangerous. This was Neil's father's punishment style. Of course, there was no component of filial love in that moment, I was a stranger to him and the normal restraint a father feels when punishing his child wasn't there. He could have lost his composure completely and kill me.

"Look at the floor, it's that old linoleum. Underneath it is older asbestos tile, so they decided not to pull it up at all. He talked about encasing it with another layer, but then we'd have different levels between this room and the others, so he said 'Let's not solve it,' that's what he said, and here it is, he's gone but the floor is here, just the original."

The sink had a slow drip, and it has eroded the enamel. The white gave way to a narrow ring of blue around the erosion, then to silver, then to rust.

"This now, this is important," he said as pushed me in front of him down the hallway and into the bathroom. The bathroom looked new, as if it had been redone most recently. It was very nice, frankly. Tasteful.

"They completely redid this bathroom themselves. And Neil used to say that it was the thing he was proudest of, the most perfect thing he'd ever done with his own hands. It is. It's as good as professionally done, look at it. Really look."

He pushed me into the bathroom and down. He grabbed the back of my head, grabbed a clutch of hair and pushed my face right up to the wall. He misjudged something, and my chin bounced off the edge of the tub. My head flooded with the taste of falling. He didn't apologize, he didn't lessen his grip.

"These aren't sheets of tiles, they're individual tiles. He put every fucking tile in here, spaced every tile, chose every next one. Could you do that? Could you have done that?"

The angry grandfather seemed to want a real answer.

"I don't know, but I certainly respect the work. It's beautifully done."

This didn't work for him. He muttered a curse under his breath and smacked the back of my head with his open hand, hard. He pointed to the wall as he spoke, "You don't get to make this like it's your own. I won't let you eat this as your own and shit it out all fucked up. This is Neil's and it will always be only Neil's and don't you fucking say word one about it to Calvert, EVER. Even if he asks you. Do you understand me?"

I wasn't sure I did, but I knew what I needed to say and that is what I said and it was "Yessir, I do." He seemed to be running out of steam, I was thinking that I might not be forced into a crawl space to look at footings or into the attic to appreciate insulation. I'm not sure why, but I said, "I'm sorry, Sir. I'm sorry about Neil and I'm sorry about how weird this is. But I'm only trying to help Marissa and Calvert. I'm trying to give Calvert just a little more of Neil, as best I can."

He didn't like this either.

"The closest thing Calvert can get to Neil is me. I'm the closest there is. Neil didn't have any brothers, so it's me and then it's Calvert; that's it."

"Yes, absolutely. I'm just trying very, very hard to do what Marissa wants well, to be as true to Neil as I can in every way. For Cal."

It came to me then that his name was Gavin, but I didn't know whether I should use it. Probably not. To call him Gavin would be too far distant, and Dad is obviously way too close in. Just Sir for now. Maybe just Sir always now. He was slowing, his anger was tiding away. He moved back, stood down, turning.

"I don't know how Marissa can stand this. You're just haunting them."

He walked out of the bathroom, and I heard him talking to me from outside the room. I couldn't understand him, and not wanting him to escalate again, I hurried after him. As I came out the door, I saw him turning to me, talking, saying "it's going to end badly no matter how smart she thinks she's being. It's going to be worse than it would have been if she'd never done all of this. She's a sweet girl, she does mean well, but she didn't think this through."

I wanted to do the moment correctly. My mind reeled through discussions I'd had with Marissa about how Neil responded to things, how he dealt with conflict, his style of arguing with her, and how he was at work, and I netted out of that an understanding that he would be silent, that it was the time to say nothing because any words would just shrivel and it was Gavin's space, and so I let him have it. If Gavin's son Neil had been there, well, it would not have been the situation, Gavin would not have been in that state. But if Neil had been with Gavin in a similar state, he would have had the means to comfort his father, he would have had things on which he would draw, and he would have been able to engage this pain with a counter, but I didn't have that. So I reconfigured the thought and imagined for a moment if Neil were *exactly* in this, if he had somehow been me—a single man who had grown into acting and responded to a certain ad on a certain day—and I had somehow been him—a successful man with a beautiful family who died too young—and Neil had been here with *my* father who was horrified and haunted and Neil needed to know whether to speak words to him or to let him have the air fall silent around him, to let the sunbaked dust of the home shroud him and leave him in the peace of his agony, and I think he would have chosen as I had done, he would have watched the man in silence and humility and even shame and wondered how he would finally lay me to rest for my boy's memories.

12

Jessica is leaning closer to Jeffrey in the living room. She is sharing a joke with him. He closes his eyes as he chuckles, smiles, tosses his eyebrows. Marissa and I have just completed the clearing after dinner, finalizing the move from dining room to living room.

In the far room, Cal and Sam are squealing and chasing one another. They are playing a game of their own invention, and the rules and objectives are unclear to all but the two of them. They know each other's limits and preferences, though, so it's exceedingly unlikely that things will spiral into yelling or crying. This is why their parents are relaxed; calmer than they almost ever get to be anymore. They are drinking wine, joking, well beyond the formal small talk of parents who are forced together by their children's friendships (but who don't really like each other), this is actually a little exciting, it feels almost like actual friendships forming. Marissa and Jessica are commenting on this to one another and Jeffrey jumps out of our discussion of David Lynch movies to link up our separate conversations.

"Yes! I was just thinking how hard it is to form friendships as an adult, and they always glom on from other things, other sources. Your kids, or your job, or your neighborhood, or your building or other random things. It's never like it was when you were a kid."

"But," Marissa counters, "when you were a kid it was just the same. It was about your school, or your locker, or your neighborhood, or all the same random things. There's no magical source for true friendships, they always just come up out of circumstance."

"I remember when I first met your brother—that's how we met, I was friends with her brother first," says Jeffrey, in full raconteur mode now. "And there was this morning after he and I'd been doing some stupid awesome thing, I don't even remember what, and I distinctly remember thinking 'Eddie and I are gonna be friends a long time, we're gonna be old middle-aged dads bitching about our kids and jobs and wives to each other,' and then not a week later, we're out being stupid awesome again and there's this gorgeous girl who comes walking right over and while I'm still trying to figure out what I'm going to say to her when she gets to us, she slaps Eddie upside the head and it's clear they're siblings and, well I mean, c'mon. Too perfect."

As Jeffrey says the word "gorgeous," his face changes, he grows younger, and a glow of real happiness rolls across him, his recollection of falling in love with Jessica replays over him physically.

"Well, it wasn't too perfect at first, now was it, Honey?"

Jeffrey blushes slightly, "No my dear, no it wasn't."

Jessica is up now. They have just handed the baton off, and she begins her leg of the story.

"Eddie was kind of pissed after we got together. He complained about how now he couldn't talk to you." Jessica is telling the story to Jeffrey, they are on stage together. "About who he was fucking, or stuff he shouldn't be doing, stuff he wouldn't want a family member to know about, because you might mention it to me, and *you* couldn't talk to *him* about who you were fucking because . . ."

She shuddered with theatrical disgust,

". . . it might be me. Ohmygodohmygodohmygod."

I feel a little surge of something as Jessica talked about fucking and did her great shudder. I didn't know where it came from, it wasn't conscious. I sought and found a thread back into the conversation. To Jeffrey I said, "So you got out of that with a friendship and a family. Twofer. You and Eddie still close?"

"Oh yes," Jessica says, "they're thick as thieves still. Really they're the only good source of trouble either one of 'em's got."

"We have a standing thing once a month where we clear out of town to somewhere and blow off steam. It's really essential to my mental health at this point," Jeffrey says.

"Which means," Jessica says, picking up seamlessly from her husband, "my brother and I are Jeffrey's one-stop-shop for both adding pressure to his life and releasing it."

"It's like you guys just wrapped him in to your family," I said, feeling vaguely jealous.

Marissa says, "Really, aren't all families that? They're lines of blood relations that keep pulling in strangers, pulling in friends."

I feel another little surge now, and a little hot shame for the prior one. I think about Calvert suddenly, wonder how he and Sam are doing in the next room, what they're both up to. I consider getting up to look, but then I hear them, I hear their quiet conversation, I hear him run and retrieve something to show her, and I know that they're good and that it would be a bad time to interrupt. They make a little burbling noise that everyone in the room can hear.

A beat. Then Marissa says suddenly, "We have a little summer place up north, a little cottage. We would love to have you guys up there this summer if you'd be willing to join us."

This is not something she and I had discussed. But upon hearing it, I love the idea, and I want to kiss her for suggesting it. I say these thoughts aloud.

Marissa smiles beautifully, and walks over and kisses me, more warmly and sincerely than she has ever done. She alights beside me on the couch, takes my hand. Jessica and Jeffrey seem to like this idea too, and they both smile without hesitation and I can tell that the answer is yes and that this thing will happen.

13

Calvert is sitting asprawl his little chair with his little legs folded oddly, it doesn't look like it could possibly be comfortable, but it obviously is. He's looking at a book on his lap, and there is a second book getting its spine broken between his side and the arm of his chair, and he has a toy—I can't tell if it's his elephant or his stuffed Thomas—tucked on the other side. He does this, he gets lost down a tunnel of thought or dream and pulls new objects into it, pulls their pictures or paragraphs or physical shape into the deep and winding tunnel he's digging, and so he ends up surrounded by a pile of toys or books or pamphlets from which he'll suddenly break and head off to do something else, or be pulled out of by his mother or me. But still in it now, deep within it, he is bobbing his head in a way that intends to show thoughtfulness. I suppose it may be the way I bob my head when I speak to him, and thinking about it, I realize with some embarrassment that it is.

I have gone down tunnels just like that to get here, I sat with Marissa's tapes and binder-clipped sheets and photo albums doing the same thing, projecting myself somewhere just beyond where we all live every day. He is out beyond the short, clear outlines of the real world, he is out beyond where it drops off to endlessness beneath, out where everything is possible, where the storylines from the TV show intersect with the roadside blur, where the impossible things that fate has closed off are reopened from the other side, where the things you have lost are unruined and returned to you, where the click of everything falling into place is loud in your ears, loud enough to make you look up and see your father there looking at you with wistful love.

14

"So Neil, what's up with the pipe?" Jessica asks me as she absently attends to Sam's attack on a hollowed-out bagel.

Bright, cold sunlight falls in the window of the coffee shop, through the steam and thick smoky smell coming off the grill hidden somewhere deep in the back of the place. Not too many people here on a weekday late morning; a couple of salespeople, maybe a realtor there preparing for a meeting in a booth, a pensioner at the counter, and our little playdate foursome at the coveted window table.

"You know, I don't have a great explanation for it," I say, spinning and weaving, "my father was not a smoker ever," recalling now Gavin's handful of my hair taut against the back of my head and my chin against the tub and the taste of falling in the center of my head, "but my grandfather was, and somehow it just seemed like a civilizing thing. It was a thing you did to punctuate the day with little breaks, you'd take a walk and enjoy a bowl after a meal, or while you were waiting for a thing. It takes an empty space and fills it with something warm and aromatic and a little fidgety in a satisfying way."

"When we talked about smoking back at Gymnasticks, I didn't realize that you were an active smoker now. It doesn't seem like you. It doesn't seem genuine."

Now I'm far enough in after all this time, that I don't really remember being out. It doesn't feel fake. But something about those two little sentences put me on edge. I felt for a moment like she knew everything that I was pretending and that she was trying to let me know that she knew everything. She was right; she had cut to the fact that when I used the pipe I was not being the person I grew up from, I was being Neil. It was a very Neil thing to do and a very "not me" thing to do. I had not thought about this until just now.

Jessica was somehow able to see the gap between Neil and the me I had been originally, before I'd been Neil.

"It's genuine for me now. There was a time I wouldn't have believed I'd do it, but now it's very real. Isn't that how all these grownup things work? All the things that are 'acquired tastes'? None of them has raw natural appeal, none of them is like an apple at the first bite. They all present as kind of shitty and a little rotten or dead, but then you move through the stuff that's initially off-putting and you find something wonderful there. Whiskey or blue steak or tobacco or caviar."

She was going along with it, she was giving me this.

"I know what you mean. Like a thing you *want* to like, and even though you don't at first, you keep on until you do? The wanting to like it carries you through the place where you would otherwise stop, right past the things that would turn you away at first? I had that with yoga. I *hated* it at first. I couldn't do any of it correctly, and the instructor always seemed to be correcting me more than anybody else. And it hurt. All the beautiful people who seemed to do it effortlessly neglected to mention that sometimes it kills you the next day. The friend I went with was a natural, after like the third class she was saying 'Oh, I love this, I might want to become an instructor,' and I was thinking to myself 'Are you shitting me, this is like going to the dentist.' But I wanted to get to that place where my body was doing something good while my mind was doing nothing—that's what they promised on the tin and I was like 'Goddammit, I'm getting some of that' and that kept me doing it even though at the end of every session I was like 'That sucked.' But now I really do love it. I got through it."

"And now you go to your friend's sessions in her beautiful studio?"

"No, it's funny, she's kind of tapered off. She had that flash of loving it, but then she couldn't keep it."

"Amateur."

Jessica smiled in that calm sainted way and I felt like I was watching spring happen. Sam and Calvert were drawing on the same place mat, one of them had moved it to a position between them, and they were each working in from an edge toward the center. Their drawings were oriented 90 degrees apart from one another, since they were sitting at the corner of the table. Their drawings were extending into each other's regions, their little arms wound around and past each other, their lines and shadings warped and wefted and somehow the intersection of their images seemed angled the right way no matter how you looked at it.

15

I didn't know the phone number when it rang. The man's voice was familiar, friendly, but I couldn't place it for a moment. Then he clarified, "Sorry, Neil. It's Jeffrey."

Jeffrey was not somebody I had spoken to outside of the strict context of both couples together. I was not accustomed to the idea of speaking with him if I could not picture Marissa and Jessica in the next room also talking. There was a gap in this situation, it felt a little odd, almost inappropriate. But I brushed the feeling away with a smile and hearty good fellowship: "Jeffrey! Good to hear from you. What's up?"

I expected that this might be a call to plan our next grownups night together, or our next daytrip with Cal and Sam. But that was not why he called.

"So I'm sorry, I should know this for sure, but you are in risk management, right?"

I'd generated some casual patter on the topic, because I knew I'd need it. I'd read some stiff books on how it's supposed to be and then lots of articles on how it kind of works, and then even more forum posts on how it actually worked. And of course, I'd have to make it a little sarcastic to make it real.

"Yep," I responded, "I'm all about dreaming up bad things before they happen. And crushing ill-formed dreams. Why do you ask?"

"Well, I'm struggling with the risk management group here and I'm looking for some objective external advisement. Nothing formal, but just your judgment. I'm sorry, is that inappropriate to ask?"

"Depends. Are you just looking for ways to argue your point internally, or do you want to be able to go back to your people and say 'Here's a professional opinion that slaps yours down'?"

"Well, definitely the former. Maybe the latter."

"Okay," I said, "give me the details."

"Alright. First, I have to say this, this is entirely off the record, this is all shared under personal NDA, right? Doesn't leave this phone call?"

"Yes, of course, of course."

Jeffrey proceeded to describe a situation that made little to no sense to me.

"Okay. So we've got a transaction where we're angling for controlling interest in a foreign utility-provider that's licensed locally, but the valuations are all over the place because of FX volatility, and what's even worse is that the local licensure requires us to have a majority component of the transaction in local currency or local equity, so obviously my RM team is trying to manage the terms and it's totally bogging down the discussion but see my thinking is . . ."

I felt the slightest tickle of panic. I had no idea what he was talking about. I would have to beg off based on specialty.

"Jeffrey, I have to stop you. This isn't my area. I don't do financial risk."

"But just let me walk through the scenario with you. I'm looking for broad strokes about the international component, not so much the financials specifically."

"No, Jeffrey. I can't. I don't know what you're talking about. I don't even know what the terms you're using mean."

Jeffrey made a small sound on the other end of the line.

"But you do political risk, right?"

He had me on this. When I was reading up on risk management, I had to find one that made sense to me. I had to find one I could internalize. I liked the political risk one, I could dramatize it easily, and it sounded boring to most listeners. But apparently Jeffrey knew more about it than I did.

"Isn't foreign exchange risk and overseas local licensure all right in your wheelhouse? Isn't that what you do?" he asked, almost pleadingly.

Now I was in improv territory. I acknowledged this to myself, forced myself into the mode, "Yes, and while I've got some good colleagues who know that, my angle is much more about electoral fraud and the human factors."

There was a dismayingly long pause on the line.

"Um, okay, is there any chance you could connect me to one of your 'good colleagues' to help me with this?"

I could hear the air quotes. This was going poorly.

"Oh, Jeffrey, I'd love to, but that couldn't be done over our 'personal NDA,' and you'd have to engage them formally. You'd have to hire us."

"Okay, you know what, I think that might be the way to go."

Oh shit. Oh shit.

"Sweet," I responded, "let me get my sales team to put a preliminary proposal together, and then I'll have them reach out to you?"

"Do you have enough for a proposal? I mean, you said you didn't understand what I was saying, what will you tell them the proposal is for?"

"You'd be surprised how often we start with really vague scope," I bullshitted. "I've got enough to start this."

"Well, okay," Jeffrey said, sounding skeptical. "We're trying to close this out in the next two weeks. Can we get this happening before, say, Wednesday of next week?"

It was Sunday.

"Oh, yes. That won't be a problem at all. Our work always comes in hot."

"Okay, thanks, Neil. I really appreciate any help you can provide in this. I'm in a bit of a spot and really need the help."

He recited his email address and work phone number and his title, and I pretended to take it all down. As I did, I was already planning how I would forget. It's the only approach I could use, forget about the discussion, and if things were really moving as quickly as he indicated, he'd need to find other ways to deal with it, and the problem of engaging my company would just go away, and I could apologize and we'd have a great new joke about my shitty memory, and the incident would be behind us. This was my plan A and there was no plan B.

16

It was painful on Marissa sometimes, the urge to make it right. No one saw this more clearly than Matriosha, Marissa's sister.

Matriosha—Matty—had been different towards her from that first birthday party where Neil "returned." That day Matty had been frozen at first in shock, then slowly over her in minutes grew a creeping panic, a horror at what she was seeing. It was an undoing of a beautiful thing. She had always had strong ambivalent feelings about Marissa and Neil; she loved how beautiful their relationship was while yet she couldn't help but be envious of it. His death had been a cold hollow terror that also freed her from the envy, made the envy sad and petty in remembrance, and opened her to love in hindsight her sister's marriage. To love it like a tragic art.

But then not even a year later here appeared this hideous employee of Marissa's, a cheap doppelganger to whom she was paying Neil's life insurance money in order to fool her child. She was executing a fraud on her only child and destroying Neil's memory with a bad imitation. And Calvert didn't know. Poor little Calvert. He was so sweet and innocent and the fraud was undertaken with such skill that he was completely fooled. It was horrible in a way her imagination would never have conceived possible until it was there in front of her in the cheerful primary colors and sticky hand prints of a child's birthday party.

Across the years of it, her sister was lost in this obsession that burned in her like a smoky cinder. As if it were her job. Matriosha looked it up once, "urge to make things right," in the half hope that it would be a diagnosis, a flavor of OCD for which there was a curative spell or powder she could procure for Marissa in defense from it. She found only "tisiphomania," a "morbid obsession for righting an injustice through means considered taboo or inappropriate." The name was derived from Tisiphone, one of the three winged furies that haunted and punished those who had committed wrongs. The treatment was talk, and so Matty knew it was hopeless. She tried though. Through half a dozen delicate conversations, she found the name of a specialist who dealt with this condition, and carried her name and address on a folded post-it in her purse for weeks until she could talk to Marissa about it.

It went as poorly as could be expected. M and M railed at each other with a freedom they had with nobody else. Marissa patronized and lectured because in her eyes Matty was always oversimplifying and had no stamina for long or involved projects. Of course she wouldn't understand this exercise, or would see it incorrectly. From her side, Matty was trying to cajole Marissa out of her hypnotized state; Marissa got like this, she would get so wrapped up in a scheme that she lost all her bearings and went to a place that was a little scary to observe and was far removed from reality. She seemed a little crazy. They talked past each other, they danced around while each had patience to do so, they gave ground on minor points in the hope of making more progress in the long run, but finally they grew tired of the positions and their caring scarred over. There was no buy-in to the project from Matty, there was no talk therapy for Marissa.

No, Marissa believed her own process would be the better treatment.

The not knowing if her methods were correct, if she was doing it the right way, was a part of it. Marissa knew that great things, that large noble endeavors, contained within them many tiny horrors and disturbing ambiguities. The challenge of a great project was staying with it, bearing on through. She focused on what worked. I was good at being Neil, she had done well to select me and my instincts were sound, and Calvert had what she had hoped for him to have out of it. But sometimes after talking to Matty, even she could catch in the corner of her eye that maybe it was all wrong, an elaborate device that may be destroying what she hoped it would preserve. A restoration of a painting that obliterated the original. She made peace with this fear and put her head down and moved on. She focused on the work, she planned and re-planned the endgame and this carried her past the doubts, every time.

17

We were on a whiskey tour, the three of us; me, Jeffrey and Eddie. It was Jeffrey and Eddie's outing, but they had asked me along. At our third stop, I was looking at the whorled bottom of the tumbler as he asked me the question. I held the glass to my lips a long time, wishing with half my mind that I could dive into the cool ripples of glass trapped in the bottom of the tumbler, thinking back with the other half of my mind to how I had stepped into this particular trap.

Jeffrey had invited me nonchalantly one night when the four of us, both couples, had been out to dinner together, having left a single babysitter to watch Cal and Sam together at J&J's place. It had come up very organically, Jessica had ordered a drink that she found objectionably sweet and Jeffrey had tried it and noted that it was the bourbon that made it so, and then I asked if I could taste it. I liked it. This led wanderingly to a mention that Eddie and Jeffrey had a whiskey tour planned, a trip one night through several bars that specialized in obscure and arcane whiskeys, and that I should come, that it would be fun, and that a fresh perspective would be good to break open their old-friend-I-know-what-you'll-like foregone outcomes.

I could admire how smooth a setup it had been. When it was suggested, I was completely unsuspecting. It was done in the manner of all our couples' time together, open and honest and obvious. The invitation into the close friendship of Jeffrey and Eddie was something like miraculous, I had never considered saying anything but yes.

And then there I was staring across an oily ocean of amber at the thick curls in the glass, as Jeffrey said, "You don't work at AON, do you?"

I put down the glass and looked at him. I considered saying many things, responses rang in my head but each disintegrated when I tried to pick it up. I was not afraid to look him in the eye, and I did, but did not speak. I saw his face, it was confident, expectant. After a long stretch of this silence, I saw a brief flash of fear in Eddie's eyes, but it passed. Jeffrey broke it with a smile.

"C'mon what's the real story?"

"What are you talking about?" I asked coolly, trying to buy time, trying to buy information.

"Neil did work at AON, but he died in 2001. You either faked your death, or you're not him. What's the story?"

Of course, he had called the Political Risk group at AON and asked for me or had dropped my name to the bizdev person and somebody told him about Neil's death. Of course. He wasn't going to wait for me to generate a proposal or have a salesperson call him; he was going to start it. And now here we are.

"My bet is that you're not him, because you don't really seem to have the patter. I don't think you actually *know* risk management."

Eddie moved over between us, forming a triangle with me against the bar, up against the server station. It wasn't a threatening move, it seemed more like he was protecting Jeffrey.

So here was my great entrance, here was my cue to take the stage and deliver the soliloquy.

"It doesn't matter who I am that way. I'm Calvert's father. That's the only thing that matters to anybody, to me or to Marissa or to Calvert. That's who I am. I'm Neil, Calvert's father."

Eddie's brow furrowed. He seemed annoyed. "What the fuck are you talking about?" he asked impatiently. "That wasn't the question. Are you Neil or are you somebody pretending to be Neil?"

Jeffrey gave Eddie a little side-eye. I had given an answer, and Jeffrey had heard it, but Eddie wasn't picking up.

"Yes. I'm both. Is that what you want?"

Eddie looked like he wanted to hit me, but Jeffrey was not angry, Jeffrey was pulled in. He asked the next question:

"You weren't always both. Were you Neil in high school?"

"No."

"Who were you then?"

I suddenly felt very protective of my birth name. I felt like the person I was before Neil was a fugitive who had escaped to another country, and I needed to protect him.

"No," I say, "that's not a thing we're talking about."

"Neil," Jeffrey said, kindly, openly, leaning in towards me, "I feel like we've become friends, like we've had some honest, real conversations about things, and so this is a thing I need to resolve. Unless you want this to be how it ends." He sat up suddenly, "I feel bad if this is the way it ends for Samantha and Calvert, because they're really close, but my little girl needs to be safe, and this doesn't feel safe."

And that brought the color to my face and I felt fear, real fear up my back.

"No, okay. Okay. This is very simple. I am playing the role of Neil. Marissa hired me to make sure that Calvert has memories of his father. I'm an actor and I play Calvert's Dad. That's the truth."

"So you're actually his stepfather?"

"No, I'm not. I'm portraying his biological father, I'm actually being Neil.

"Well, you're pretending by using a false name, but Calvert knows you. You are the person he loves."

I was becoming a little confused. I felt like this was confusing the issue.

"No, you don't understand. I'm playing his father. The things I do are the things that Neil would have done, not what I would do."

"But you're the person he knows as Dad. You're his stepfather. You're going to pretend to be Neil for the rest of his life? How is that going to work? He's going to find out."

"I'm not going to be around that long. Calvert's Dad is still going to die when he's a boy."

Eddie looked angry again. Jeffrey looked sad.

"What? When?"

"I don't know for sure. Look, Marissa has been very clear on this from the beginning. When Neil died, Calvert wasn't even two. He would have had no memory of his father. She hired me to be around and to keep Neil alive for Calvert for at least a couple of years until he would be able to remember. She has a plan for how it ends, but I don't know and I kind of don't want to know."

"That's fucked up. That's cruel."

"No it's not. It's no different from what already happened. Neil is dead, it's just that . . . word of it hasn't gotten to Calvert yet."

"But you're letting him grow up with you and get more attached to you and it's going to be so much worse for him this way. If it had just happened when he was two he wouldn't really have known the difference."

"Look, I love that boy. Are you telling me that everything I do with him is wrong? That I shouldn't be doing this at all even though he likes me here, and his mother likes me here? That's fucked up. It's not your place to say that."

"But you could be you. He'd love you the same. Why aren't you just you? And what is your real name?"

"No, that doesn't matter, it doesn't enter into it."

"See, now that bothers me," Jeffrey says, leaning back. "I think that concerns me most out of all of this."

"What?"

"That you have to hide who you really are. This whole playacting thing is weird, but the fact that I don't really know anything about who you are is the worst thing here. That's the thing that makes me protective of Sam."

Yes, that made sense. Here was a grown man he thought he knew as the biological parent of his daughter's friend, but it turns out he's an impostor, he's some other person entirely, and how scary is that shit? I could be a serial killer. I'd have to tell him my name. I sighed heavily, I was good and fucked.

"My name is Derek," I said, and this was true. "Derek Robards." This is not true; Robards is not my last name.

I don't know why I gave him the name of my friend from fourth grade, but I did. I couldn't give him my whole real name because I'd need that after Neil died, and I'd need to not be somebody that Jeffrey or Eddie could look up and find after that point, because I'd need to not exist. So I lied, and as I said it, I felt it curl deeper. I felt like I took another step down into a spiral that just went down to some tight little constrictive point.

"And so at some point in the future, Neil is going to die—somehow—and you're going to go back to being Derek Robards and forget all about Calvert and Marissa?"

"No, I'm sure I'll never forget about them. But yes, I'll go back to being Derek." That felt very strange to say and I had the sensation of being in one of those nightmares where you find yourself naked in public. This segued oddly into Jeffrey's next question.

"Have you slept with Marissa?"

This question annoyed me for some reason. "Well . . . we sleep in the same bed, but we aren't intimate."

"Oh, well at least *that's* like a real married couple," Eddie said. He didn't smile when he said it, but this was the first hint of levity Eddie had shown all night. Maybe something was finally turning. Maybe I was reaching the other side of this. I wanted to give Jeffrey something more.

"Jeffrey, Calvert and Sam are kind of a special pair when they're together. They're particular friends. We agree on that, right?"

"Yes," he said, skeptically.

"Well even with how strange this arrangement is, one of the things that I feel good about is that he will have that to comfort him when I'm not there. He'll have that still."

I let that hang a moment.

"I take this very seriously, I'm not fucking around here. This is my job, my only job, to be the father Neil would have been if he was here today. And apart from the name, I'm not faking any of it, I'm not faking my love for him."

"How old was Cal when Neil died?"

"A little more than a year, maybe eighteen months."

"Derek, I've got to break it to you, you're his real dad. You've been doing this, what . . . twice that time, at least, right?"

"Please, please don't call me that name. Please don't. I'm Neil. Please do this for Calvert if not for me."

Jeffrey rolled his eyes slightly and looked a little exasperated.

"Neil, do you see what I'm saying?"

"Yes, I do, I totally get what you're saying. But that's not what this is, and there's no converting from what it is to what you're suggesting. That would totally destroy the point of this. It would be worse than if I was never here. And this is not my call to even be talking about this. This is Marissa's call. Okay, let's stop for a second, I want to talk about this now. I don't want you knowing this to fuck up the whole thing. I'll need to tell Marissa that this happened, and I have to hope that she doesn't just pull the trigger right then. Oh fuck. FUCK."

I was by that time quite terrified and feeling too much. I was losing control of my responses. My eyes were wet. I felt like it was all collapsing. I'd fucked it up just because my research wasn't good enough. Oh fuck.

Eddie said "Jesus," and left for the men's room.

All this seemed to change Jeffrey's tenor. He reached out to my shoulder.

"Neil, Neil."

I just keep cursing quietly. It was kind of hard to tell how much time passed.

"Neil, let's just go talk to Marissa about this. Nothing has to change right now. It's better if it doesn't. I'm sure she'll agree. Let's just go do this. Hang on."

He got up and went to the men's room. He and Eddie returned and stood next to me.

"Ed will keep it here, okay?" Jeffrey said to me, making a circle between the three of us with his finger. He turned to Eddie, "Thanks, man. I'll give you a call. Thanks for this. I owe you."

Eddie smiled at Jeffrey and said "Hey, of course." He turned to me and put out his hand, which I shook. He just said "Neil," and then made a little shrug with his hands and said "I don't get it, but you seem to really care, so, you know . . ." and he shrugged again and then left, patting Jeffrey on the shoulder twice as he walked out.

18

Jeffrey was right. Marissa did not pull the trigger.

When I unlocked the door she called out to me from the couch, not looking, and then something made her look up to see that Jeffrey was coming in with me, and she straightened up a bit and then got up quickly. "Jeffrey! Did you have to escort my boy home from the tour? Did he overdo it?"

Jeffrey smiled and said "Hi Marissa," in a neutral way, but then she looked and saw my face and it must have somehow conveyed that some horror was afoot, and her mood came down a notch and she said "What's wrong? Are you okay? Did something happen?"

I had no strength left in me for nuance or subtlety, and if Neil was to die tonight, I wanted it to happen quickly. "Jeffrey knows, he knows the whole thing," I blurted out.

Marissa's first instinct was to look to her left, down the hallway towards Calvert's bedroom. Then she looked hard at Jeffrey, with a really steely glare, a mama bear kind of thing. It was frankly a little scary, and I think Jeffrey was surprised to be on the receiving end of it, but he had no malice in him for her, and he said "It's fine, everything's fine. I'm not going to mess it up. Let's all get on the same page."

He walked past her towards the couch and I just dropped my coat on the floor, and as I followed I leaned close to Marissa and said "I'm sorry, I tried not to," and she made a little tight-lipped face and we all went and sat in the living room. Jeffrey opened it.

"So a while back I called AON on a work-related thing and I dropped Neil's name and that seemed to make the people I was talking to very confused. Then after a few of these confused people, one of them told me he had died, and so I knew something was up. So tonight Eddie and I asked him about it and didn't really give him an out. So this is on me, I'm sorry. Neil tried to keep it under wraps, Marissa, but I wouldn't let him."

I felt a little surge of affection for Jeffrey that he chose to call me Neil and not Derek right now.

"Okay," Marissa said, guardedly. "Apology accepted. So what are we talking about now?"

I remembered now where I'd seen this steely Marissa, and it was when we'd had that conversation about me re-upping and I talked about compensation and she got this way. This was what she looked like negotiating from a corner.

Jeffrey was calm but kind. "I just wanted you to know, and to know that I'm on board to play along. Calvert's a sweet boy, and Sam loves him and I don't want any of that to change any more than you do or Neil does, so I'd rather we just keep everything the same. I know that's up to you, and frankly Neil here was afraid that you'd end the whole exercise tonight when you found out I knew. And that's up to you, you're running this thing, but I just wanted to say that I really, really hope you don't choose that because I think things right now are really great. It's rare when a person can perceive that they're in the midst of the good old days, but I think we're in the thick of them right now, and I'm in no rush to change them. I thought it was important to say that to you myself, and I couldn't let Neil come here without doing that, because I was half afraid he'd have a heart attack."

Marissa listened and was quiet for a moment after Jeffrey finished. We were all quiet. I thought about saying something, but I couldn't think of anything that wasn't an apology.

"Are you going to tell Jessica?" she asked.

"You'd be putting me in a really bad place if you asked me not to. Jessica and I don't have the kind of relationship where we keep secrets from one another. But for what it's worth, I'm confident she'd feel the same way I do. We like you guys, and we love to see the kids together. So yes, I'd be inclined to tell her."

"Can you get her over here now?" Marissa asked, all tactical now. "No, never mind, that's stupid, she's home with Sam while you're out. I'd like to meet soon, the four of us. I'd rather tell her myself."

For some reason I said, "Can I tell her? We're going to Gymnasticks tomorrow morning, and I caused this whole thing and I feel like I should clean it up." To Marissa now, "I told Jeffrey, and see how he's on board. Let me do it."

"With the kids right there? No, that's not a good idea. The last thing we need is either of them overhearing something or asking something, oh that would be a fucking disaster." She swiveled back to Jeffrey, cursing under her breath.

"I can't ask you to wait, she'll ask how tonight was and you'll have to lie and probably suck at it. You'll have to tell her. Show me how you will tell her when you get home tonight. Pretend I'm her. Tell me. 'Hi Honey, how was the pub crawl? Were you and Eddie nice to Neil?'"

And while they both playacted, I stopped for a moment and breathed, knowing that this was not the end.

19

The next morning was Saturday, when Cal and I woke early per our habit and breakfasted quietly together before class. Scrambled eggs with bits of ham, tea for me, warm Ovaltine for him. I was distracted, not least because I had misplaced the pipe. I had chosen not to bring it out with Jeffrey and Eddie; that would have been too precious to indulge in their company alone, so as I'd left the house last night realizing I didn't have it I turned that realization into intention. But today was different. The sunlight over the kitchen sink sidled through the window differently, the nest in my head where I kept who I was and what I was doing was more open now, it was stretched and there now it showed the impression of Jeffrey and I imagined also that of Jessica, and I felt opened and cold. I felt an aching desire to hold the pipe, I wanted it in my pocket, I probably wasn't even going to light it on the way to the class, but I felt a pressing need to have it in my hands, to have its stem tucked between my index and middle, with the fat warm bowl nested in my palm. I checked my coat pockets, but it wasn't in any of them, and I checked my dresser and the hall table, but it wasn't there either. I was checking stupid places, places it would never be like the fireplace mantel and the drawer under the side table where there was never anything except two little marble coasters lined with cork. Then I saw it across the room. It was on the lower shelf of the end-table, it was down where nobody would have put it other than Calvert. The pipe was a little smudged on the stem and bowl, it showed signs of having been handled by small greasy fingers. I had never told Calvert not to touch it, there was no prohibition to his picking it up and trying it and playing, and so it appears he had, and then put it on the nearest convenient spot after his performance had been rendered.

What they said last night was true, I was real to Calvert not just as the role I played, but as a physical father. I had driven this role forward from the beginning with a specific method: what I knew of Neil was the framework, the whole structure was built around the things I could be sure of, the things that were unambiguously Neil from photo or anecdote or Marissa's recollection. The way he tilted his head to smile at those he loved, the way he opened to conversations rather than commandeered them, the songs he whistled absently, the kind of fabrics he preferred, the books and music he liked, the things he wanted for his son. Those were the components I was sure of, the only ones I could always be certain on. These things required no thought, no further consideration as to whether they were a correct choice or the best for this little boy to see and model from; they were Neil's so they could not ever be a misstep. Working within this framework, the rest could be filled in without all too much consideration. The rest was water to the fish. Unnoticed, unconscious, invisible. Who remembers what he did last Tuesday at 2 p.m.? Nobody, and nor does anyone remember what their father said last Tuesday at 2 p.m. But the smile meant for you, that you remember; the laugh at the silly kid joke you made, the music listened to, the habits revisited each day; these persisted. These were the framework of the person in your head, and to know that some of my own choices and decisions and preferences might slip in amongst Neil's was not so much a concern. But it did mean that what Calvert remembered of his father was partly me. There was no purity here, there was no perfection; the parts that had been my choice to do and which Neil might not have done, these things might perhaps be the stain on the true, but this was the only way Calvert would get any Neil at all, and that was the entire point—a goal so great and true and heartbreakingly desired by all parties that all the unintended consequences were worth bearing, without question, without question.

Perhaps Neil would have lost interest in the pipe by now. But it appeared he had not, and so neither had Calvert. I leaned down and picked it up from the lower shelf of the table as I called to him then, sing-song in the way I did, but quiet enough to not disturb his mother. He fussed because he was settled into some distraction, but after a joke to wheedle him away, we were off.

20

I spotted Jessica early, and then felt an anxious tickle when I looked over at her as we queued up to get into Gymnasticks. I could not bear a moment of pretending or assuming, so my first urgent words to her were "Once the class starts, can we talk?"

"Yes," she said, smiling, knowing already, forgiveness in her gentle eyes, kindness. Clearly, Jeffrey had done me a solid.

After the taiko and tumbling was underway and the children distracted into (or from) it, she came to me where I stood at the low wall and put her hands on my hands and looked me straight in the face and said, "You're his father, and a wonderful father at that, and everything else should be secondary. Just, that's all that matters, really. Okay? Now, let's talk," and I smiled at her and breathed again and maybe I blushed, and she made a small tight smirk and that part of it was done.

And from there I unraveled my thoughts into her hands like a ball of yarn. It was not so hard to speak with subtle coding when Sam or Calvert came over or passed by, and there was none of the fear or vague threat that I had felt last night with Eddie on my flank and Jeffrey with his ambiguous aggression right across from me. Here was Jessica in her truest form, in her most beatific and understanding mode, open with love for the liar and the sinner like a Christ in Eileen Fisher. She, like Jeffrey, hung upon the issue of Neil still having to die.

"But don't you think that the loss he's going to experience is worse than what would have been originally? I get the logic, I understand keeping a memory alive, but there's no reason why you couldn't work through that later, when he was older. You could drop the conceit today and your name changing would be easy enough for him to adjust to. Then everything would be real. Aboveboard and real. And he'd get to have his father all the way through his childhood. Wouldn't that be better?"

Coming from Jessica, the idea sounded a bit different. I considered it now really for the first time without countering it. The idea struck me oddly. It was immensely appealing and at the same time, terrifying, claustrophobic. What a joy to actually be the Dad, to wear the role not as a costume but as my garment. Yet it was a horror.

My return to my own life—the ability for me to live a life where I was not loving father next to this child for the next two decades—flew from me like a finch. But of course, it could never be.

"No, because then Neil would be totally eclipsed. It would be as if he had never existed, and that's the opposite of what Marissa wants. And this is her plan, remember, for her biological son. And there'd be the whole mess of the money, too."

"Money? Oh please, if she can make the money work for these, what, four years, then there'd be some other way to make the money work with a different arrangement. But is that really the most important thing anyway?"

"No, no it's not."

"I think you should get the secret out, be done with the faking. That's the stuff that gets worse, harder over time. It boils up bad decisions."

"But don't all couples have stuff like that? Don't you and Jeffrey have things that nobody else knows that you wouldn't want them to know? Isn't that part of what makes couples pull together? Things Sam shouldn't know?"

Marissa had a flicker of discomfort at this, but it was fleeting and she recovered crisply and was on, "Not big lies, no. Big lies are different from omissions or experiences that you don't want to recount. And this is a big lie."

Her move away from this was too smooth for my taste, but this wasn't the time. "Yeah, big lies are hard. This one is so big that, being up close against it all day, I almost can't see it."

"That's the worst. You're in the shadow of it all the time. That's the side the mold grows on."

"That's why it has to end, and then I'm out in the sun again."

"Yes and then Calvert's—"she looked around quickly and lowered her voice—"Dad is dead. And he's a heartbroken little boy with his mother comforting him."

"And his best friend is there." I pointed with my chin towards the two of them banging taiko sticks together, "to comfort him too, keeping on,"

"But his dad is dead, and he'll be angry at him. You know that the people left behind are always angry at those they lose? Even when they know it's not the person's fault, and that their death couldn't have been helped, they still sometimes really hate them for dying. He'll hate you after that. You will never, ever see him again, and he'll miss you and hate you."

Jesus, she was laying it on. She wasn't wrong, but her mercy seemed to have dried up a little. I supposed its vapor was still around us in the room, but I couldn't quite smell it anymore.

"Or . . . or you could just keep being his father, and drop the name quietly, and maybe when he's an adult you and he could talk about how it all happened, over a coffee or a fishing trip. But then you'd have a happy ending behind you, it would have been a strange thing that delivered a blessing."

"It's not my call, Jessica. If you want to convince Marissa, then maybe, but I don't see that happening. Sometimes I'm impressed by how much this is just about Neil and Calvert. It's not really about Marissa or what she wants for herself or me or if I'm doing it right or whether she or I even have a life to speak of during all of this. It's about the boy knowing the Neil who was, living in his presence just a little more, to absorb a little more of it, to become just a little more like his dad. Just that. I mean she sees it so clearly. And I know what she's trying to do, what we're trying to do, and I do believe in it. Maybe not as much as she does, but I believe in it. So while I get what you're saying, and how if we twisted it around to be a different thing, that it could be okay, it could be different but okay, I can't really imagine it happening because that loses the whole objective. I mean, at that point it's a choice between Neil and me and Marissa is choosing Neil all the time, I'm only here because she is choosing him. There's no question."

"Everyone else would choose you," she said.

I now felt myself making the same tight little smirk she made earlier.

21

Marissa threw her keys into the bowl and shucked her jacket as Cal ran down the hall to the kitchen. We were back from a family day out in the country. We'd driven out to take a hike in the woods, at a nature preserve, an estuary with raised wooden footpaths and wildlife at each turn; wading birds, muskrats, very briefly a glimpse of a fox, turkeys, deer. Afterwards, a lunch in a little restaurant, and then a long drive back home where she and I talked while Cal slept.

After the reveal to J&J, it took some time for Marissa and me to get back to normal. She wasn't exactly angry, nor disappointed, but she was a little tighter for a while. She was a little on edge like she was waiting for something. On the drive back we spoke in amputated sentences, understanding each other, but maybe not.

"We're still doing the same thing, right now aren't we. We're *both* still doing the same thing, right?"

"Yes, of course."

"Because it's the right thing, it's a really, really good thing to do for him."

"There's no question. It's good for him, and for us."

"I don't know about 'us.' I don't know. I think this is a time that is different than it looks, but that's okay."

"What do you mean?"

"It would be like one of those immigrant stories where from the outside they looked so integrated and comfortable in their new Americanness, but inside they were always a mess of loyalties to the old and to the new and it tortured them, and they were in hell."

"Are you in hell?"

"Not in hell. But yes, sometimes. Aren't you?"

"Not hell, no. I can flip it on or off, but I just leave it off because it doesn't belong on."

"Is it hell when it's on?"

"No, it's just scary, and it's a mistake. It feels like a crazy idea that you don't allow because when you allow it for a little while it never gets less crazy, but it does get more real, so you just flip it back off."

"It's going to be really awful at the end."

That hung out there for a moment.

"I know. But what can you do? It will be really awful at the end either way. It's always awful at the end. Then after a while it's less awful, and then after another while it's okay. Either way."

"Yeah. Yeah, that's true. You're still stuck with it being life."

"Right."

The highway ran under bridges and the sky had clouds and when the sun was behind either you'd feel the chill in the car, it would sweep over you like a cold current in a lake, and then the cloud would pass or from the bridge we'd emerge and the light would change back and then the warm current would come, sometimes in a shallow touch just beneath the hair on your arm, and sometimes in a hot press like a feverish hand on your skin.

There was more sun on her side of the car sometimes, and she would open the window a crack when it got too warm, and then close it again. There seemed to be no way to stabilize the temperature.

I began to brace myself when I saw an underpass approaching. I stored up warmth, I pushed the warm blood to my skin to fight the cool in a battle just beyond my skin. I would not fight it in my flesh. Marissa did not watch the road, she did not anticipate, she watched out the side window at the river the highway ran alongside, and she was caught by every change. At least once I saw her shiver out the corner of my eye.

After we got home, after she tossed her keys and took off her coat, she went right to the bathroom and I heard her draw a bath that I had to imagine was very hot and deep.

22

Sam was over for a Saturday playdate. Marissa and Matty had gone out to some all-day art film experience, for which they'd packed as if going on expedition: water and granola bars and fruit and wipes and in Matty's bag a small thermos of black, sweetened espresso. They'd be home late after giving their all to the artists vision. Jeffrey was elsewhere, I assumed with Eddie or perhaps doing weekend work with an actual risk management team. Jessica and I were going to make the day of it with Cal and Sam. We did Riverside park and then the children's museum and a jaunt downtown and then back by evening.

It's hard for these children to know that this is not necessarily the normal pace of the world, that it's not for everyone New York City all the time, that it's not people from every country on earth and a card-swipe and train ride to anywhere and every new idea in the world rising up through the subway smell and spilled food and fog from sprayed-down sidewalks. They have it so good, these two little children, hand in hand and so sure of the steadiness of the world's spin.

We got them back, exhausted and a little hangry, to our place as shadows outside were longest and lowest, doubling over into dusk. We whipped up some old reliables, Bell & Evans chicken and a veggie rice mix they both liked, and fed them and set them in front of a Pixar friend and they were slumped together out cold before the plot had even crested. We ordered some Indian food for delivery and cracked a bottle of Rioja.

As we ate, Jessica flipped idly through a magazine and I, looking over the little pair slumped on the couch, said "Look at those two. Wonder twins, deactivated." As this registered with Jessica, I saw it again, that little instant of something dark across her face, a flinch, a twinge. It was the same as the time at Gymnasticks when we first talked about how I was Neil, and it meant something.

"Hey, what was that?"

"Hmm, what? What was what?"

"What were you thinking about just then?"

"That there's no way the substation qualifies as an historic place. I mean, c'mon, look at it. Somebody's getting greased." She held up the magazine and showed me a photo of a nondescript brick building.

"No, when I was talking about the wonder twins."

There it was again.

"Yes! That, right then."

"What?"

Oh, she did not want to talk about it. This was something.

"Jessica, c'mon. Don't fuck with me. You get this little look like you're in pain for a second. What is it?"

She tried to laugh it off, "No, it's . . ." and then she clearly struggled to come up with something, but couldn't. She was wrapped around it, she couldn't get past it, there it was. But even at that, she didn't want to talk about it. She glanced back at the magazine with the dim hope of finding a way out through its words and images. I reached across the counter and moved the magazine away.

Very gently I said, "Hey, hey. Seriously. It's just me."

She struggled, there it was, close to the surface. Her face was active with twitches, she sucked her lips in and breathed deeply through her nose.

"Okay, give me a second, okay?"

"Sure, yes of course."

She composed herself, she was composing the story, she was framing some event some knowledge some understanding in a way to share it with me, and it wasn't simply done. I could see that she didn't want to explain it incorrectly, to say the wrong part first. This gave me time to think back to when I'd first seen it, and then it seemed to me that it had been about Sam, it was darkest when she was thinking about something Sam didn't know or wouldn't know or shouldn't know.

"It's something you're scared for Sam to know."

Jessica cried out a little bit, it leapt from her throat and she looked over at the two of them sleeping and seeing that they had not woken up, she put her glass down and got up and headed down the hall suddenly, to be farther away from where they dreamed. She may have been crying, I couldn't tell. I followed her down into the dark, turning on the hall light as I passed the switch.

At the end of the hall, she turned left, randomly it seemed, into a darkened room. It was Calvert's room. She sat on the edge of his little bed. The room was twilit, from the hall light, and I did not turn on the bedroom light. It felt like it would have been too aggressive, too much an interrogation. I stood for a moment, but then as she began to speak, I sat on the bed next to her.

"Sam was born to be a twin, when she's with Cal she's a twin again. The wonder twins. It is a wonder."

"What do you mean?"

She took a deep breath and began. "When I was pregnant with Sam, on the first visits, on the first ultrasounds, they saw twins. And we were scared, because having twins for your first pregnancy is a lot, you know? It's hard on the couple, couples having twins are more likely to divorce, and it's more complicated for pregnancy and delivery. And part of me," she grew pained again, "part of me wished when they first told me, I wished they were just a single baby. And I didn't really wish it, you know how you can have things that come into your mind, and maybe you like the thought a little but you push it out and you can tell yourself you never really thought it?"

I nodded.

"Well, I remember wishing they'd been just one baby, and immediately thinking it was a horrible jinx to think it. But it was too late and something had listened and I got my wish."

"I'm sorry. I'm sure it's not . . ."

"It's got a horrible name, do you know what they call it when that happens?"

I shook my head.

"'Vanishing twin.' Vanished. Poof. Like a funny magic trick. It's not funny. And see, the thing is they don't vanish. Well, I guess sometimes they do, but not Sam's twin. There was no vanishing. Sometimes the 'vanishing' twin stays there the whole time, keeps the other twin some kind of company, and see that 'vanishing' twin doesn't fight for their space, so they get squeezed by the other twin who is fine, who is just fine and healthy, and instead of vanishing they get crushed right between that big healthy twin and Mom's body, and then they get delivered, and on that day, well here's Sam and here's Sam's twin, here's . . ."

"Oh god, I'm sorry Jessica. You don't have to . . ." I started to say. But she did have to.

"Neil, have you ever been walking in the springtime, and you're just so happy that the cold is gone and winter is done and it's starting to feel warm, and you're happy to be outside, and as you're walking you see something on the sidewalk, and you can't tell what it is, so you look, and you still can't tell, and you get closer and then when you're too close you realize it's a tiny bird, a tiny little thing that must have fallen out of a nest too soon and then wasn't seen and got . . . crushed and is flat like a picture of what it was before? Neil, that's what happens. But it's your child. That's what I thought of that morning, a little spring bird on the ground. Jeffrey was wonderful, but I remember his face, and I saw Sam's little twin there, and he . . ."

She stopped talking. I couldn't think of anything to say that didn't seem stupid or obvious. I put my hand on her shoulder. She was no longer really able to keep herself together.

"Sam's twin was a boy. They were fraternal twins. So, that's why. The wonder twins."

I still couldn't find words, but she seemed to find something that was enough in my face. She was crying, and I touched her face to wipe away a tear and I held her face for a second, and then she leaned in and rested her face into my shoulder. I cradled the back of her head against me and gently stroked her hair. We didn't move for a long time.

We said nothing more, and the sadness had its time with us and after many minutes it began to pass and was replaced by something else. And after that happened we still didn't move for a long time.

Then Sam's tiny voice said from the other room, "Mama?" and Jessica started and put her head up and wiped her face and looked at me, looked me deeply in the eyes and said nothing, and her face seemed to say a million things and I knew what all of them were because yes I knew what all of them were, and then she put her hand on mine for a second and gripped it tightly and then gently, so gently, let go of it and her fingers brushed along my hand as she got up and walked out saying "Sam, honey, Mama's right here!"

I watched her shadow decline down the far wall of the hallway and disappear into the floor and I stayed on Cal's bed for a few minutes before I too went out and started clearing dinner away.

23

All the dozens of tiny windowed doors of the post office boxes reminded me of an automat every time. Every week when I'd go pick up my mail, all the mail addressed to Derek, I'd silently, almost unconsciously think of the automat with its little windows into the foods, into the sandwiches and the slices of pie and the bowls of soup, now all gone. We all miss the automat now even though we thought it was kind of old and stupid when it was around. But anyway, in the post office, when I looked through the little windows, some part of my mind was always surprised to see paper through there and not the corner of a plate.

That day in the box was the annual letter from the management company that ran the building where my old apartment was. It was the annual rent increase and lease renewal letter. The increase wasn't bad, $50 a month more, and there were no surprises with it, no announcement of the place being turned into condos, no removal of services, just please sign and return with another $50 for the security deposit. I looked at the letter for a long time and felt like I didn't think about anything at all. Then without emotion I checked the box next to "I will not be renewing, and will be vacating by June 30th" and signed it and put it in the envelope and posted it right there in the post office.

Now this wasn't part of any grand plan I had. I hadn't decided that I'd stay and be Neil until Calvert went off to college or that I'd be escaping to Bolivia in a year, or anything. It was just clear that I wasn't going to be returning to the exact Derek I'd been before, that wasn't going to happen. And that apartment had become, in the last few times I went to it, just an old place that I'd known. Like my room as a child growing up. It was a place where I'd lived, and where I'd been a version of me for a long time, but to which I had no real desire to return. More than once I'd thought that it was stupid for me to keep paying for it when I never used it and see that I wasn't really sure when I would return to it. Back at the house, I called Moishe's and rented a storage unit in Queens and planned a day in June when I'd meet the moving guys as Derek and let them box all that stuff and take it away. Then imagining it, I saw myself throwing a lot of it away. The stupid side table, the tired bed and mattress, the bookshelves and the books I'd already read or never would read. The cheap kitchen furnishings; dull knives and thin glasses and plates and plastic-handled cutlery. All just out. What even would I keep? I'd keep the trunk with the papers in it, school papers and yearbooks and diplomas. I'd keep the team t-shirts and a couple of those inscribed books and scripts. I'd keep the tapes I couldn't play anymore because I didn't have a machine right now. I might have a machine in the future. Those were the things I'd keep. The rest could go. I called a charity and scheduled them to come to the apartment the same day as the movers. All at once. After all the planning and scheduling was done, I decided to head over and look at the place in person to account more fully for what I would discard and what I would keep. I wanted to have it in my head before that day. I took my jacket and my pipe and headed out the door. It was warm enough for just a light jacket, but still cool enough that a warm pipe would make the walk even better.

The bowl of the pipe, when I look at it closely in the sunlight, is a tiny world, I see in its walls layered cliffs of compressed time. It's the story of a million campfires and winter hearths, each layer of char and of ashy scale is a recording of a day, of a walk, of a break from work, of a satisfying meal, of a conversation. Of days and nights.

A talented archaeologist could work backwards through its layers and identify the particles in each, separate the lonely bits of toner or the beef-fat vapor or the red wine aromatics or the leaf mold or the spring pollen and document each layer and in this way recount the better part of my life. I am buried in it.

24

Marissa and I went up early to open up the house. It was only my second time seeing it, and it would be our first time there together. I'd told her long before about the time I went up by myself, about running into Gavin and though I'd glossed over some of the interaction, the bottom line was that she knew I'd been there. We didn't speak about my prior visit on the drive, but the fact of it was present to us the whole way.

Calvert was with us of course, and he was distracting himself in his customary manner in the car, by alternating among a small cache of things he'd brought. Today the items were: a reference book about airplanes, some photos he had worried with creases, a post-it notepad, a small Lego vehicle of uncertain design and intent which had become his favorite, and a mechanical pencil which he seemed to prefer to fondle rather than to use. His method would be, while reading his book, to scrawl arrows or other symbols onto a post-it, then slap it into a page, adjacent to some airplane of particular interest to him, for easy later reference. His book looked like a doctoral student's primary reference, a source for his own thoughts spiraling out, off to their own ends, silent unexpressed, outgrown in his head by the next batch of neurons founding and connecting and entrapping the habits and images of his mother and father and his friend Sam across his every day.

I never shared with Marissa what Jessica had told me. It was not a thing that seemed up to me to share, nor would there be a context where it made sense to mention. The withholding felt a little odd, a tiny bit duplicitous, but somehow with regards to knowing it, I felt like I owed more to Jessica than I did to Marissa. I kind of felt this way generally, when I let myself think about it. I rarely let myself think about it.

We had been on the road for some hours when Calvert saw it. He said at first, "Daddy, is that a hawk?" and he pointed from his car seat up between our front seats, out the windshield. His sharp little eyes had seen the tall wings at the center of the James Farm Road bridge. We had often on drives challenged each other to find the red-tailed hawks sitting atop the light posts and at the side of the highway—to be the first to call them out to others in the car. I would usually see the ones at the side of the road, the ones working on some prey they'd downed, the talons holding down the rabbit, the beak dipping to rise again as it tore up the flesh. Calvert from his seat could almost never see those bloody hawks, but he would always be the first one to see the hawks sitting serenely on the light posts or wheeling in the sky, he would see them far sooner than me, he would sometimes see ones that never entered my range of vision, ever, and the existence of which I would have to take for granted by his witness.

"Those are the very big wings, Cal," I told him. "They are very big and they stay there almost all the time."

"*Almost* all the time? When do they go?" he asked.

"They stay right there until they need to do their work, and then they open up even bigger and flap and fly off into the sky. They always come back, though. Nobody knows what they go off to do, but they always come back."

"Noooo," Calvert said in the way he did when I'd said something silly.

"No, it's true," I said, very deadpan. I held the look and met his eyes. Calvert's silly smile faded and he grew serious. Then he bent over and craned over his shoulder to watch the wings pass above us on the bridge. He twisted around in his little seat and gripped the seat back to watch the wings recede. His contortion looked awkward, almost painful, but he held it so that he could see.

Marissa angled her head up to watch him in the rear view and then back to the road. She did not look over at me.

"Oh Honey, we're almost up to the helicopter factory! It's just ahead!" Marissa said brightly as we came in view of the Housatonic bridge above Sikorsky. As she said this, Calvert began to turn his head, but his eyes did not leave the wings and even after the statue had been eclipsed by the landscape, he did not look away for several moments so as not to miss the flight of the wings rising above the crest of the hill. When he was assured that they were not aloft, he turned brightly and to his mother said "Where, Mama?"

25

So we arrived to the stale dusty summer house and did the things that were done; we took off the storm windows and opened the windows, opened the water main with the long crank down into the hole and then let the brown water out of the toilet and sinks until it ran clear and gold-flecked in the sunlight, we vacuumed and swept furniture and floors, we washed and rinsed sinks and dishes and kitchen counters and tubs, we unpacked the bedding and made the beds and put the towels on the chairs in the bedrooms. As we made our bed, I asked Marissa "How many times did you and Neil do this?"

"All of them," she said.

"How many?"

She took a beat. "Six."

"Is this right? Are we doing it the same way?"

"Yes, of course it's right. This is the way we've always done it. It almost feels exactly the same."

"How often did you have guests?"

"Oh, just about every year. That's really why you even bother having a place like this. To have people here, to share it. Neil's parents liked to come, and Matty always brings . . . well, has brought a . . . stream of boyfriends through, too. Neil had some college friends up once, but afterwards he said it was different with them, and he'd wished he hadn't asked them, and we never had them back."

I was watching Marissa closely through all of this. This opening of the house had occurred often enough, had been a regular enough thing, that there was tradition and habit driving her actions. But there had also been the years of my project when we had not come, when Marissa must have thought about it, perhaps wanted to, perhaps was afraid to, I don't know. I kept an eye for where her head was. There were expectations here, ones that she might not remember to articulate. There was some danger here I wanted to avoid, but I do my job, I needed to know more.

"Did you intend to retire here? Was that part of it, too?"

She thought on this a moment. "I guess so. Kind of. We sort of imagined it that way sometimes. Like we'd talk about how we'd like to do the same walk in the winter or, I don't know, I liked to imagine getting up really early with coffee down on the dock and not have to count the days left in vacation, just to have the coffee and the dock and the minnows and the sun just normal every day. But at the same time, we would also talk about it like it was going to be a big family house, and Cal and his wife and kids would learn how to open it and we'd all get together as a family here in the summers, which kind of assumes we're not living here, but we all just gather here. I don't know, really, if we ever had any real intention of retiring here. Do people retire anymore anyway?"

"Yeah, people with money do. You could have. You still could I guess."

"No, I like the idea of retirement, but if I really think about it, it horrifies me. Even here. Maybe especially here. I wouldn't know who I was."

"You'd be who you are now, just not going to a job every Monday."

This was not a good thing to say, I could see this right away.

"Oh thanks for the advice. So is that your trick? How you find your authenticity?" she asked, with an edge to her voice. I seem to have stumbled into a bad place.

"..."

Marissa threw a pillowcase at me. "Just remember that you're borrowing this. You get to live this by accident. I could have put all the insurance money into a trust and just been done with worrying about this house or how things would go or any of it."

I recognized that this was one of those times when it's best to just shut up and let it play out. I busied myself with stuffing the too-large pillow into the case. The fit was wrong and I distracted myself with it. After a brief pause, Marissa started up again, under her breath at first, but slowly growing louder.

"Money is what they give you when you have nothing left to care about. It's supposed to somehow make things better. And I remember actually thinking that what I really wanted was for Neil to be here for Calvert and the phrase 'money won't bring him back' occurred to me and I thought, 'Well fuck that, maybe it kind of can,' and so here you are. But *you* are not retiring here, and whether I do or not probably won't depend on whether I'm spending that money on you being Neil. But even if that's true, it's probably the better way to spend it. But don't . . ."

She shook her head in frustration, not finding the right phrase,

"Don't like it too much. Don't like it differently than Neil would."

I'm not sure I knew what that meant. I'm not sure Marissa did, either.

26

Matty arrives first, she pulls up in her little silver SUV and an overly affectionate man bounds out of the passenger side and meets her at the front of the car and hangs all over her like a sloppy coat. She seems happy with this, they're in a good early stage of their relationship. Matty looks beautiful. She's happy and smiling and does not look fearful at all. Until she looks up at the house and sees me, and then a small shadow passes over her face. She pushes the smile back on.

"Hi Neil!" she says cheerily. "This is Robert."

Robert bounds up the porch steps and shakes my hand heartily and claps me on the shoulder with the other hand. He's entirely too much.

"Neil, great to meet you! Matriosha has told me so much about you guys. Thanks so much for having us up!"

"Welcome!" I say. "Glad to have you here. It's the whole reason we have this place."

I glance over at Matty to try to understand what she might have told him. Her face tells me nothing. I'm going to assume Robert doesn't know the arrangement and proceed accordingly. Marissa emerges from the door and walks past me down to Matty, whom she embraces for a long time. They talk quickly, quietly at each other's shoulders. Marissa wheels, cheerily now, and strides over and hugs Robert.

"Robert, welcome to the cottage. Glad you could drag my sister up here to see us. You know, it's not really summer until there are at least two cars in the drive, so you've officially started summer, too. Thanks for that."

As Marissa is speaking, I feel a sudden need to locate Calvert and be with him. Glancing through the front window, I see him in the front room and go in and say, "C'mon buddy, come meet Aunt Matty's friend," and I pick him up and put him on my shoulders. This is the easiest way to pull him from whatever he's doing without protest. He loves riding shoulders. He loves having to watch for the top of the door frame and he touches it and ducks under it as we come out. Robert greets him very loudly and cheerily, in the way that adults who aren't often around children will sometimes do. Cal wraps his arms around my forehead more tightly and I can feel him ducking down behind my head a bit.

"Hey buddy! You must be Calvert! Your aunt Matty has told me so much about you! It's really great to meet you." Robert approaches me too closely, being totally focused on Calvert. He wants to shake the boy's hand or do a fist bump or something, he's not sure what, and Calvert can't free a hand without potentially falling off my shoulders, so he just ducks down further behind my head and balls up one fist and holds it out in front of my forehead. Robert fist bumps Cal's tiny fist and bangs it hard into my forehead, strongly enough that I feel a momentary surge of rage and have to suppress a reflex to kick Robert in the balls, really hard. I don't. Marissa winces but Matty and even Robert don't seem to notice.

"Daddy, can we go to the lake?" Cal asks from behind my head. My blessed child, deliver us from evil.

"We should help bring in Aunt Matty's and Robert's things first, buddy, that'd be polite," I say.

"No, no, no. Absolutely not, I insist," says Robert, "I've got those, you guys go."

"Thanks, Rob," I say. I want to see if Robert is fine with my shortening his name, mainly to see if he's as relaxed as he presents. He seems to be, he smiles and nods urgently and claps me on the shoulder yet again as Cal and I walk past him.

"We'll see you in a bit, guys," he calls after.

I walk down the lawn to the road with Calvert still on my shoulders and I stop and over-dramatically check the always-empty road both ways before crossing. As I do it, I say "Left. Right. Left," as I look each way, turning my shoulders to cue Cal to do the same. While I'm doing this I push from my imagination the horrible subconscious movie of him running across the road to the lake, not looking, the car coming fast, too fast to swerve and hitting him and tossing him far down the pavement, doll limbs flailing, then lumped lifeless. As I look left and right and say the words, I feel the jerky motion of his little head swiveling, looking each way.

"Any cars coming?" I ask him.

"No cars, Daddy."

We cross and he leans forward, putting his little chest against my head, wrapping his arms under my chin. I am the trusted horse. The lake is bright and calm, with small ripples unfurling far out beyond the wind shadow of the shore. The sandy bottom is transparent golden, and minnows dart around the pilings of the dock and in and out of its shadows. I'm in shorts and flip-flops, so I just keep walking, I walk directly into the water, splashing loudly until it is up to just below my knees. Calvert had not been expecting this, he is surprised and a little scared, his horse proceeding straight in. He is excited and I bobble my shoulders a bit as if my footing were unsteady and he might get dunked and he squeals "Ah, Daddy! Stop!" and I do. He is relieved, the false peril has passed now, and we just stand silently on the shore together for what seems like a quiet lifetime.

27

Cal and I are still down at the lake, on the dock on our stomachs, looking over at the fish, when J&J and Sam arrive.

"Sam's here!" I say and Cal is up and on his feet and then running towards the house. He stops—good boy—at the road and waits for me before crossing, though he is vibrating with excitement.

"Hey guys!" I shout across the street as they step out of the car. I nod to Cal to signal it's okay to run across and he runs right up to their car, and begins tugging at the back door of the car to get to Sam. Jessica gets out with something in her hands, some kind of basket, housewarming I guess. She slings it onto one arm and we embrace. It's just a hug hello. There's nothing else to it.

"I'm so glad you guys could come." As I say it, I swing my greeting across J&J and then down to

Sam as she jumps out, then I step back and call to Marissa to let her know they're here. Sam and Calvert run off into the house. The screen door smacks like a rifle-crack and that will be the sound of this weekend forever. I walk around to Jeffrey and shake his hand and we pull in for a shoulder-tap hug. "This is quite a spot," he says, appreciatively. "Thanks for inviting us."

"Oh my God, it was meant for this. This is going to be great," I say. I'm vibrating with excitement, too.

Marissa comes out and we do the needful and begin loading their stuff in and up. Earlier Marissa laid out the plan for who would have each bedroom, so I lead the way to their room and put their bags down. Marissa gives them the tour of the house and all the while Cal and Sam are unnoticed, unattended except by each other, safe, happy, and noisy.

Matty and Robert had decided to "take a nap," so their room was not on the tour. The noise of the arrivals "woke" them, though, and Rob emerges in the last stages of pulling on a shirt as the rest of us are descending the stairs. Matty calls something from the door that he closes behind him. He follows us down the stairs, and Jessica, who is last down the stairs before him, can't quite decide whether she should stop awkwardly on the stairs to greet this strange man, or whether she should just continue down. I feel the need to help the situation. I say aloud, so loudly that it's clearly directed at Rob, "Good nap, Rob?"

Rob seems pleased to find me addressing him; he is beginning to feel like he's "in," he engages heartily. "Hey Neil, oh my god, yes. Nothing like country air and quiet for a good deep sleep."

We all reach the first floor, and I introduce everybody all around. "Jessica, Jeffrey, this is Rob. Rob is here with Matty, Marissa's sister. Who is apparently still asleep. Rob, Jessica and Jeffrey are our good friends from the city, our kids introduced us."

All greet one another, and I want to say "Now we're all here," but Matty isn't here yet, and thinking back I know that Matty probably hasn't met J&J yet, and an additional introduction will be necessary, so no, we're not all here. We are not all here yet.

28

The bed here is smaller than the one at home, and during the night I cannot untangle from Marissa. There's always a limb touching, always some contact. It cycles between sensual and annoying all night long, and I wake repeatedly, either excited or angry. Upon the last awakening, I see that the sun is just up and I get out of bed and pull on yesterday's clothes and go downstairs.

Everything is quiet, nobody else stirs. It's very early, and everyone was up fairly late last night, so I expect to be alone for a couple of hours. I wander the house, gathering glasses from the living room. Dishes from dinner, still unwashed, are piled in the sink. I gingerly unpack the sink onto the counter and begin the washing, which I realize will take several sets; the dish drainer cannot hold it all. Realizing there is still stuff out near the grill, I head out to gather that up as well.

The air outside is just enough cooler from the house that I feel it down the back of my loose shirt as I gather a couple of glasses from the porch and the utensils and an empty plate from the grill. The only sounds are birdsong and the distant whine of a car on the state route on the other side of the lake. The lake throws brightness back at me, blindingly. I turn back towards the house and there is Jessica at the top of the steps.

"Hey," I say. This feels oddly meaningful.

"Hey," she responds. This, too, seems significant.

"This is alright, isn't it?"

"This is very alright."

She regards my hands full with plate, tongs, glasses. "Can I help?"

"Thanks, no, I've got it. Well, actually if you can get the door." She opens the screen door for me and as I pass by her I say "Thank you. Washing dishes is a 'chop wood, carry water.' I like it, and I'm a little selfish about it. But thanks."

She follows me in and moves the remaining dirty dishes on the counter so there is room for what I'm bringing. "Okay, I think I'm going to take a little walk down by the water, then. See you." And with that, and the lightest touch on my elbow, she is gone.

I locate an old, thin dishcloth, one with cotton so ancient it contains decades of thirst, and begin drying the items I've washed already. I take particular care when stacking the dishes and placing the glasses back on the shelf; part of the challenge I give myself is to do this so silently that nobody will realize that I'm doing dishes. I hope for Marissa and everybody else to come down and be surprised by the miracle of the dishes done, as if their transition from dirty to washed and put away was a thing that just happened of itself, a natural order of events, a fact requiring no human effort or attention. Only Jessica would know, and even then, she could not say she had seen it happen. I place the next plate gently on the others on the shelf, so lightly, as though it might detonate. While I do this, my mind wonders if Jessica is wearing shoes, or if not, if she is wading into the cool lake, or if it is too cold and too early for that. My mind decides what it wants to see, and I picture her wading, shivering, becoming adjusted to the temperature, then relaxing. The dish drainer emptied, I start on the washing of the next set of dishes, and my mind washes them in the lake, in my mind I am at the lake a few dozen yards away, not here in the kitchen, but there. Now I am being at neither place fully, really.

29

The morning stalks me slowly, too large to see; it advances without me noticing. I'm finishing up the second batch of dishes. I expect that Rob will either be down first or last, and when I see Jeffrey round the corner, I know Rob will be last. I nod over to the large percolator that's ticking and puffing on the counter and say "Coffee?" and Jeffrey says groggily, "Good morning, yes, please."

Marissa is close behind. She puts her hand gently on the back of my neck by way of greeting, and queues up behind Jeffrey at the coffee. "Good morning, boys. Jeffrey, did you guys sleep okay?"

"Like the dead."

"Jessica still asleep?"

"No, she's up and about somewhere. Neil, you see her?"

"Oh, yeah," I say, "she's off by the lake I think. That's where she said she was headed."

"Walking across it, no doubt," Marissa says, almost inaudibly. Jeffrey involuntarily smirks and lets go a small amused snort.

"Sorry, that was . . ." Marissa starts.

"Nah, nah," says Jeffrey, "she'd have laughed too."

Last night, Jessica had seen to the children being bedded down, and then joined the adults in a single glass of wine and a brief hour of cards and talk before yawning and sweetly begging off to bed herself. We all the others stayed up and drank more and had a second round of grilling and I suspect there was some illicit smoking off at the edge of the yard near the opening forest, and in general there was a spirit of indulgence and merrymount wantonness in the night. Nothing scandalous or immoral, but a sense of teenagers unleashed, unsupervised, engaged in mild naughtiness and fun.

The window above the sink faces hard east and now it comes. The sun, which has been pushing its way through the trees all morning as if lost in the forest, has now just clambered above the highest trees, it crashes into the window like a bird, and I am suddenly squinting and unable to look out. The part of the morning that was quiet and washing of dishes in soft light alone is done. It closes like an act of a play.

I hang the dishcloth and step behind Marissa and ask "Line starts here?" and I wonder when Jessica will be back.

30

In the side yard, the ground is oddly rippled, it is thick with grass, but betrays that some kind of digging or plowing or tilling had happened not too long ago. Well, long ago relative to this moment, relative to this summer, relative to Calvert's life; but not long ago geologically, just a split-second ago relative to this plot of land or the lake or even the house. Perhaps a decade. Walking across the yard with Calvert, I notice a few tall shoots of grass that seem to erupt out of the rest of the low blades. They each end in one of those dark, bulbous tips that bend it over in a graceful rainbow.

I remember now this plant from my childhood, it's like coming across an old friend. This is how you do this: I pluck the stem and fold it over itself once, then fold it over again, perpendicular. I push the second fold up to the base of the bulb and turning it towards Cal say, "Hey, check it out," and pulling the stem I pop off the tip and it flies through the air past Cal. He blurts out a laugh at this and plucks up a stem and folds it randomly, not knowing what to do. I pluck a second one and pop it off again and it flies even further. He is really excited about this now. I pluck a third and squat down and say "Here, look." I slowly fold it, stopping at each step so that he sees what I'm doing. Then, after I'm sure he's seen each fold, I pull the stem slowly, so slowly that it seems like nothing might happen, and the tension builds. I'm holding the grass right in front of us and he is in close, and squinting in anticipation of the launch, and then just as he is beginning to think maybe it won't work this time, POP, the bulb pops off and flies straight up between us and on its way down bounces off the top of my head.

Calvert laughs and looks about and realizes with some delight that the whole field is dotted with these plants, that they pop up every few feet and that we could run around this field all day picking them and popping them off and not use them all up. Suddenly this empty yard is overlaid with new meaning, it has become a playground and a treasure room. I recognize that we're probably seeding the whole side yard with an invasive weed as we do this, as we play out here shooting haygrass tips at each other, but I could not possibly care less, and I am certain, *certain* that Calvert will never forget this.

31

The children own the daytime and the adults own the nighttime. That's the agreement everyone makes on vacations. Daytime is filled with wholesome walks in the woods and swimming and fishing and strange new stores with penny candy. Nighttime is filled with intoxicants and fireworks and secrets and fears and desires and things almost talked about but not quite.

Matty and Rob seem to be having a lot of sex. Nobody can be certain of this—they are reasonably discreet—but they have secreted off together several times, disappeared for blocks of minutes that align well to furtive fucking. They are also richly physical when they're with the rest of the group, they touch and lean and hang upon one another. This does something to the atmosphere of the house.

Sam and Calvert receive the vibe as prankishness. They suddenly are a team that likes to play tricks on the adults. Jessica cannot find her keys when she is intending to drive to the market. They are not where she left them and she begins looking silently and it's only when she asks aloud whether anyone has seen her keys that there are giggles and the adults know what's happened. The cap on the milk is left loose, and Rob is showered when he hefts it from the fridge. After he cleans the floor and himself, he quietly locates the salt shaker and tightens down the top which had been set the same way. The adults realize that the remainder of the time here will be sown with minor traps and giggling collusion. The adults are surprisingly okay with this, as if they somehow felt the same way themselves.

The locale obliges all this perfectly. There are neighbors encountered by the shoreline once or twice, but they seem more content to keep to themselves than to engage beyond niceties. They feel the cohesive vibe of the eight in the little cottage. They are attracted and then slingshot away by the gravity they create. Boats on the lake hum and bark the call of their own bands of family. At the store, all buy the same charcoal and meat and veg and wine and some imagine the subtle differences of that group's revels against their own, imagine the guards let down and trod upon like handmade rugs.

32

The nap in the afternoon is what had done me in. We'd all agreed that the big meal of the day would be the afternoon grilling and after the prep and the eating and the clearing, and perhaps influenced by the effects of a few summer-style beers, I was overwhelmed by exhaustion in late afternoon. J&J had taken the kids by car to some local attraction, and Rob and Matty had also driven off to somewhere or other, and Marissa took to a book. I took to the bedroom and yielded to a damp sunny sleep.

When I awoke, it was getting rapidly dark. I had somehow slept not a nice thirty minutes but hours. I was a little surprised that nobody had disturbed me, not even the prankster twins. I heard the voices downstairs and felt a rush of pleasure. I would rejoin them and it would be laughter and jokes, but first I could take my time in the quiet and dark, and go down when I was good and ready. I lay and listened to the voices and laughter for some time before I got up and went down.

The leftovers from the earlier grilling were now being enjoyed cold from the fridge and foil, and some sort of new grain-and-veg salad had been provisioned and was out on the counter for self-service dishing. Coming into the brightly lit main room, Jessica sits crossways on Jeffrey's lap, with a plate of something in front of her. His arm is down the outside of the couch, his fingers loosely gripping the mouth of a beer bottle half-resting on the floor, angled. A great peal of laughter emerges from the group just as I round the corner, the slim trailings of a story still winding from Jeffrey's lips as he brings the beer up and relaxes before his audience. Jessica reaches her hand around and lovingly rubs his hair and the back of his head as if in reward.

Jeffrey glances over at me and pauses before taking a sip of his beer, exclaiming "Van Winkle!"

"You damned kids making your racket down here!" I say. "A man can't sleep!"

Marissa, whose back is to me, turns and smiles and I walk up behind her. She leans her head back and I lean in and give her a great kiss on the lips. We linger an extra moment or two in the kiss, just long enough that I feel a tingle along the length of my torso. "Welcome back to the world, sleepy," she says gently, very close to my face, after we part.

From the corner of my eye, I see Jessica's head turn away as I stand up from kissing Marissa. Jessica's hand does not leave Jeffrey's hair, but cycles slowly, gently through it. Matty and Rob are nowhere to be seen. The front door is open but the screen door shut. In quiet moments, the sound of moths casting themselves against the screen becomes audible.

I ask J&J where they went today, and they recount the local town they visited, its mill-turned-art-museum, the falls, the dam, the ice cream, the history walk. They share fresh the small moments that make such days memorable: the piece of art that was made of nothing but pens and pencils held together by unseen forces, the tiny window in the mill's cupola that looked across the valley to the fire tower miles away, the crazy stacks of driftwood caught seething in the teeth of the dam, the fallen starling nest on the paint-flaked ground with a tiny blue egg hinged open and yellow-faced nude nestling laying still nearby, the woodchuck in his rippling run across the dam's broad angled grass apron, the sideways clank of the stilled waterwheel against the permanent current. All during the retelling, Calvert is playing with some hand-hewn toy J&J apparently bought him today, and Sam is sleepily eating berries and thumbing through a coffee-table book of scenic vistas that looks to be 1960s vintage.

The cold grilled chicken that Jessica is finishing looks very good to me, and I go to the kitchen to get some. As I load a plate, Matty clatters in through the back door, through the kitchen, and leans against the doorframe into the living room to announce "The lounge is open if anyone would like to join us," and as she passes back through the kitchen she makes a quick joint-to-lips gesture to me as she exits again.

Jeffrey follows out after a few moments, and Marissa heads past the other end of the kitchen to the bathroom. After a few minutes, she emerges and then heads out the back door as well. I pull a cold beer from the fridge, pop it open one-handed on the wall-mounted opener above the trash, then pick up my plate and go back to the living room, even while the bottle cap continues to work its way down loudly through the objects in the trash can.

Jessica is in the chair now, and I half-sit on the arm of the chair to begin to eat. We greet each other as if I had just come down from my nap now, with "Hey" answered with "Hey." After the first sip, I stand the beer on the end of the arm where it looks somewhat precarious, and after a moment, she picks it up, takes a swig, then wedges it between her leg and the edge of the chair so it won't fall.

From where I half-sit, I can see out the back screen door, and there, tiny in the black panel of screen, I think I can see little flickers of orange light, briefly bright, then almost imperceptibly dim; perhaps imagined. I think how I must look from there, how bright the house looks, like a little diorama, with a sliver of kitchen and then a doorway, and beyond me leaning on the chair, eating, talking, sipping.

I think what might be going through Jeffrey's head if he is looking in. All the thoughts from the day, and now with a beer in him and a smoke coming around to him, what kind of whole thing his mind might be. What floats up.

"What was his name?" I ask Jessica.

"Whose name?" she asks, but as soon as she finishes asking, she knows who I mean. She looks up at me, oddly. Not angry, not sad, but as if waiting for me to explain why I would ask this now. Why I would ask this here.

"I'm sorry, I shouldn't have asked that. I don't know what I was thinking. I'm sorry."

I'm watching Calvert negotiate a twist of the wooden puzzle. He is not so much solving it as just turning it in his hand, becoming familiar with its ways. Maybe that's all solving is.

"It happened too early. We knew too early. There was never a name."

Some part of me wants there to be a name, wants to know it, and before I can stop myself I ask, "Not even in your head? Just in your mind?"

"No. How would I have even done that? That would just be extra pain. No."

She shifts the topic now to Calvert who continues with the puzzle. She tilts her head towards him.

"You have a little puzzle master there. He figures things out. He likes the figuring. So if you want to talk about names, Neil . . ."

"Yes?" I say, not entirely getting where she's going with this.

"How about Derek? That's a good name, don't you think? Should that be the name in my head?" she says.

I'm all turned around now. "I . . ."

"Of the one who isn't here?"

I must be wearing a strange expression, because Jessica's look softens, and now she says "Sorry," and rubs my leg.

Sam, who has been falling asleep looking at the book, slumps and the book falls off the table with a loud thump. She is startled awake, and Calvert looks up from his puzzle and smiles and laughs. Sam's expression begins as wide-eyed shock, but when she hears Calvert's laugh she looks at him and chuckles to herself softly.

"C'mon you two. Let's off to bed," I say. I put my plate on the table and escort them up and see to the jammies and tooth-brushing and bed. A story is a necessity, so I read, pro-forma, through a brief book Cal has heard dozens of times. As I read, I hear happy shouts and giggling from outside the house. Someone's running, now others. They're having a hell of a time out in the dark.

Sam is out quickly, but Cal is not sleepy. He says as much.

"Just because you're not sleepy doesn't mean it's not bedtime. Here, now what you do in this case is lay in bed quietly and think about the day and listen to the grownups being silly downstairs. That's what you do on vacation. See the light that comes up from the stairs? See the big triangle of light on the ceiling? Like a pyramid out in the desert." A peal of laughter drifts up from the window. "Hear that? Now, goodnight little bear. See you in the morning."

I occupy Calvert's mind for several long moments as I descend the stairs. I am there in his mind, living what I have suggested to him: I'm upstairs lying in bed with the adults downstairs, I am content and am filled with the expansiveness of life, of the new things seen today for the first time, of the potential things I will see and potential things I may one day be myself in the far-off promising future, am happy to hear the breathing of my best friend in the world sleeping just across the room, am comfortable that my father and mother are there for me, will keep the world right-side-up for me. Will continue to be.

I complete the stairs and turn the corner, and Jessica is still sitting where I left her, drinking our beer.

"Shenanigans out there," she says. I believe I can hear splashing and whooping from the lake.

"I think you are right," I say.

"I suspect they may not be wearing suits, either. Crazy kids."

"I think you're right about Derek," I say quietly.

After a beat, Jessica looks at me, very intently, and slowly a smile leaks from her tightened cheeks across her face. She gets up and hugs me, suddenly, tightly. She steps back and her face is aglow, I'm not sure I've ever seen her looking this happy. She touches my face and says one word, and then says it again, harder:

"Yes. YES."

I am happy and terrified and full of love and unsure how I will make this happen, but sure that I must make it happen.

Later the bathers would come back in, wrapped in towels and dripping, still laughing, tired. They would not, could not see the drops of water falling off them onto the dusty floor, leaving what we would see tomorrow as little clean washed spots in the dust.

33

I still end up being the first one up the next morning. I suppose this couldn't be helped, given how my head has been spinning since last night. It's a strange thing to have made a decision. There is nothing different out in the world, but yet everything is locked in a new direction. This morning being cooler, I see from the porch mist rising up from the lake, and it reminds me of my pipe. I suddenly feel an intense desire to smoke it. I get it and knock it out and then repack it and light it. This is my pipe, and my smoke. The lake has its mist and I have my pipe. I feel like a slim layer has just sloughed away between me and each of my actions, and now each thing is somehow more sincere.

Marissa's voice from days ago comes to me in my head: "Don't like it differently than Neil would." No, that will not be possible. That was never possible.

The entire morning I will be half-present, working through in my mind how I will convince Marissa. I'm not certain I can, I'm not certain I can alter the course of her project, but I know that now I have the vast and growing history with Cal to point to, that it's become a larger thing than even she can wave off. But it can't be threatening, it can't come across as a power play, as her project in mutiny; that would only make her double down and I'm actually a bit scared to imagine where she might go if pushed that far. I can't dismiss the notion that she'd just make the thing play out as originally planned. She could do this whether I go along or not. Neil is dead, his dying again would just be truth deferred. She wouldn't even have to lie.

But Calvert. Following the plan now would be worse than a year ago, and much worse than two years ago. She can't deny how it would hurt him. And she can't deny how my staying would continue to give him joy. Inertia is on my side. Her love for Calvert is on my side. Jessica and Jeffrey are on my side. But it's not about "sides," no, it's about the boy, it's about Calvert, it's about keeping his life complete and arranged in ways that will give him a better shot at whatever he wants to do. It's more for him, the best she could possibly do for him. Wouldn't she want the best she could possibly give him? This is the logic by which you sell a parent something. There's no way to remove his father from his life without it costing him. It would only serve Neil, and now what would Neil want? What would he want to happen here? I know what Neil would want, and he would want Calvert to be happy and have more love in his life than not.

I will need to feed her small slices of this argument, I will need to talk in ways that are not direct, I will need to allude to this and cause the decision to arise in her mind as her own. The will of a woman like her cannot be forced in a new direction, but it can be steered, and easily, by long subtle winds. Winds that come in from beyond the scope of her vision. This will have to be my project. I puff my pipe like industry.

We'll keep the things that I could never fully claim. The "Backstreets" magazines will be kept as artifacts, things from a beloved family member Cal didn't get to really meet. Let's do this parsing out now of what is truly just Neil's and what is shared by Neil and Derek. Derek. I think my name aloud in my head, think about saying it to Cal, and it feels dangerous and exciting, like confessing love. There is so much I will need to finesse, but the prospect excites me. I feel (for the first time in a long while, I am realizing) deeply challenged. All these tasks before me will require thought and practice and talent to execute well, and if I succeed, the end will be much like the now, but all open. There will be nothing false, and nothing ruined.

I hear small sounds behind me from back in the kitchen. Little voices, trying to be quiet. The wonder twins are up to something, setting up a prank. I hear liquids pouring. I open the screen door slowly, so that the spring doesn't creak and I ease the door shut behind me with no report. Choosing my steps carefully, I work back towards the kitchen, putting on my serious grownup face, ready to bust them. I'm too late, though. There is a flurry of whispered giggles and as I reach the kitchen they are disappearing around the corner and I hear their little feet fly up the stairs.

For a moment, the entire kitchen feels mined. I scan the counters and see nothing obvious. I test a few container tops, but all fine. What was being poured? There's a small bucket near the door, wet but empty. Nothing suspended above, no full container poised to fall. Nothing in the sink. Hmm. I open the refrigerator and nothing seems unusual there. Then I see motion. Then more.

The Brita pitcher is not as clear as it usually is, and there within the off color is the motion. Half a dozen tiny minnows dart about in the pitcher, investigating the filter, reacting to the light caught in the corners of the plastic, reacting to one another. In the bright light of the fridge, and now at eye level for the first time, I see them with unusual clarity. They're beautiful, nearly transparent glass along their bottom half, with gray and brown-amber spots, almost like tiger-stripe camouflage, along their top half.

I can't suppress a chuckle. Somehow I am proud of them pulling off another prank, and one that took some planning. I consider a moment closing the fridge and pretending I hadn't found it, but then I look at the minnows and think of them in the strange container with no sandy bottom nor sun, growing slowly colder and colder. Would they die if I left them here until someone else discovered them? Possibly. A pitcher of dead fish is not so funny as a pitcher with bright darting ones. Killing, even accidentally, would beg serious guilt or punishment, while this as it was here now could be met with a laugh and a finger wag.

I pick up the pitcher and the fish dart alarmingly. I walk straight out through the front door and don't soften the screen door's slam. I know that the twins will probably see me doing this, I bet that if I looked up to the window of their room they'd be looking down and maybe with a little sadness that the joke had such a small impact, but I'm okay with that since it impresses them with how important it is to me that the fish be released alive. Somehow that is the first most important part of the lesson. It's true, but it's the demonstration that does it. The seeing it happen is more important. So much of this parenting is the demonstration, the delivery of an idea through modeling of it, through action, only later to be reinforced by calm words, logic, empathy. At the road, I stop, and model again the left, right, left check for traffic because they watch me now and because I am the grownup. The steps from the road down the lawn and the sandy shore take forever, and it is like a religious procession. I am returning seeds of life to the source of life. I'm also just putting the fish back. Making things right, doing the right thing.

I pull the top off the pitcher and pull out the filter shelf and drop them both on the beach and wade in and gently, gently place the pitcher into the lake until the lake water spills over the lip and into the pitcher and mingles with it and the fish are swept around by its current and then the pitcher is completely underwater and I pull it away from the fish, so that the plastic walls seems to mysteriously recede, and there they are back in the lake, wide open hazy distance in all directions, and they are gone, instantly, gone. But for one. This one was maybe damaged. He wriggles oddly, turns upside down briefly and swims awkwardly for many long moments. I feel a pang as I watch him. Then somehow he regains his normalcy and rights himself in a half-Immelmann and is gone in a jet of wriggles.

The relief I feel at his recovery is surprisingly moving. A warm rush spreads behind my sternum, and I am smiling. I pull the pitcher out of the water upside down so that it's empty and I walk back towards the house, stooping but not stopping to pick up the pitcher parts as I come. I can see in my peripheral vision the curtains in their window moving. I don't look up to them. They're probably not sure whether they are in trouble or not. This is good and appropriate, for now. Later I'll let them off the hook.

34

My wife Marissa seems to be sleeping in. Others are up and about, breakfasting. Matty is off swimming with the freed minnows she doesn't know about. The kids are working on scrambled eggs and waffles that were plied from the dark crusted iron that's probably older than all the adults here. J&J are at the table with the kids, vacation breakfasting, which is like regular breakfast but somehow different. The kids have been vaguely avoidant of me since everybody got up, and I haven't addressed them directly yet. Rob comes down with bags, and piles them near the door. This is the first I realize that he and Matty are leaving today. J&J seem struck by the same realization at the same time. I had assumed that their leaving time was generally known by others, that I just hadn't been paying attention, or been present when it was announced. Maybe as they passed the smoke last night, I presumed, somebody said above a held breath "We're heading back tomorrow, I've got a class," or something like that. I presumed the in-group had connected on this. I presumed there was stuff there. Maybe not.

"Hey Rob, you guys are heading back?" I asked cheerily.

"Yeah, yeah, I'm traveling for business tomorrow. I've got a flight first thing, so gotta go back today. This has been really wonderful, thanks so much for having us."

"Oh, sorry you have to go. Does Matty want to stay and go back with us? It wouldn't be a problem."

"Oh, that's nice of you, but no. She's got a thing tonight."

This sounds like complete bullshit to me, and I resolve in my head to make the same offer to Matty directly when Rob's not there.

"Grab some breakfast before you go. There's plenty."

I'm wondering now if I'll need to wake Marissa to say goodbye to Matty and Rob. I pour Rob a mug of coffee and feel the ending coming. The ending of this time here at our cottage with the eight of us.

Matty comes in, drying off. She didn't just go wading, her hair is wet and down her back. Rob says to her, "Okay, Babe, just your dry clothes up on the bed in the room. I got everything else."

"Sorry you guys have to go so soon. Matty, Marissa's still in bed. You may want to wake her up to let her know you guys are leaving," I suggest.

The children are watching, but this is not an ending so meaningful to them. It's just the two adults furthest from them leaving. They don't have the same anticipatory nostalgia that I do, the bittersweet knowledge that this capsule of memory is closing. They haven't lived through this kind of thing before, they don't know how the remaining days will have a small void where Matty and Rob have been up until now. They don't really know loss. They have never felt time as an erosive force. They don't know that it is even a thing that happens. They are only beginning to learn to feel time pass, they are a long way from seeing it remove the earth they stand upon and drop them to a fall.

The ancient waffle maker clicks on its amber light to tell me the next batch is ready.

35

"Matty, I know Rob's got a flight, but if you want to stay on, you can come back with us," I offer quietly on the stairs.

"Thanks. No, I've got a thing tonight."

I chuckle. That they both described it exactly the same way.

"What?"

"No, it's just that Rob said exactly the same thing. That you had a 'thing' tonight."

"Well, I do," she says, visibly annoyed with me.

I'm seeing her now as my sister in-law. One that I have a little history with, maybe we always didn't get along, but my family. The person she used to be, a woman who was just on the periphery and objected to the project, that person is fading. The sibling is here. Her annoyance is not a threat. It's just annoyance.

"You two are really sweet. You're a good couple. It's nice, Matty. You guys being here was really wonderful. This was really special for Cal."

Matty softens just a bit at this.

"You're good to that boy. I don't like to think about what's coming."

"I know, I don't either. Maybe I just need to sweet talk Marissa into another dozen years."

"Maybe you do."

"Well, make sure you guys get some eggs and waffles before you go. There's plenty."

"Thanks, Neil," she says from behind me as she follows me down the stairs.

Moments later, Marissa appears silently, she pads into the kitchen. She puts a hand on my shoulder as she passes, says "Good morning," in a quiet voice, creakily.

Now more goodbyes in the slanted early sunlight and the breakfast food steam.

36

The six of us remaining banded closer after Matty and Rob left. It was to be a lake day, so we gathered the things; the semi-dry towels off the line, the bucket from the kitchen corner, the floaty and noodles, the paperback, the snack bag. The play and the relaxation by the water was freighted with a sense of value it didn't have before; there wasn't much of this left. Soon J&J and Sam would be leaving too, and then the three of us left would close up the little house and drive back again ourselves. That was still many hours away, but that number was finite. There wouldn't be other outings on this trip, there wouldn't be other trips to the grocery store, there wouldn't be any new guests arriving. The arc was curving gently downward.

But the thought that this might not be the last of these times here—that one year from now we might all be here together again, with the kids a year older, but the adults the same, exactly the same—that notion rang in my head and filled me with a secret joy. It could be so, and maybe it would be so. I could make it so.

Indeed, Marissa herself had softened into our display of marriage over the past many days here. Our being a couple full time in front of others had changed our habits. It wasn't so much a show of appearing like a couple, of trying; performing the small simple acts of married familiarity was simply easier and appropriate for Rob and the kids to see and, well, it was comfortable. It is astonishingly pleasant to be touched gently as your partner walks past you, it is a deep joy to share a knowing glance across a room, to launch into laughter at the same moment. These things reinforce themselves. At a certain point, it no longer matters how the relationship started, the pairing gains gravity and becomes a force that requires greater and greater effort to deny. Its realness requires no intent to arrive. This vacation had been a miracle, and I think back to how angry Marissa had been making the bed, and I wonder with a small pang of guilt where this leaves Neil. Where he is now.

I get up and pick up the pool float and wade into the water and say to Calvert, "Are you up for it?"

"What?"

"An expedition. To the island." I lean down next to him and point out to the wooden swim float anchored a few dozen yards offshore. I know to him it looks impossibly far away.

"Yes! Sammy c'mon!"

Sam clearly doesn't want to. She is engaged in her own project around the leg of the dock, something involving rocks and sand piles and tufts of grass. She just shakes her head.

"Sam!" Cal whines. She shakes her head, blurts out a petulant "No!"

"C'mon man, let's get this going. Hop on," and I offer him the pool float. He jumps on, nearly slides off the other side, but finally gets his balance. "Let's away."

Though the water is only calf deep here, I stoop down to get horizontal next to the cushion and get my own balance for swimming and pushing him out at the same time. He wiggles on the float and I realize that I actually need to be careful here. He could dump off when we're a hundred feet out and the bottom is ten feet down. Small lungs fill quickly. This sense of real danger makes the adventure real. This is not all patronizing silliness, adult playacting. I need to be careful, he needs to listen, we need to work together.

"Okay little bear, we need to work together. I need you to stay on the float, stay low, don't move too much. That way I'll get us there faster. Got it?"

"Got it, Daddy. Go! Go!"
"Going!"

I start swimming. The tops of my feet scrape painfully on the sandy bottom a couple of times, and after I adjust them up, I'm breaking the surface, splashing water on everybody on the beach. Everyone shouts at me, and I adjust my kicks until I've got it dialed in.

Now we're moving. Quickly, the water becomes deep enough that my swimming is genuine. Cal is settled in on the float, he is alert and focused on the swim platform. It comes towards us slowly. This is the long part of the trip.

The water temperature shifts alarmingly as I swim. An idle corner of my mind tries to pattern it together, tries to imagine the puzzle pieces of cold and hot edging against one another in the lake, tries to explain without words or science or reason why hot is hot and cold is cold, but it finds no fact or explanation and so it just sifts and sifts and sifts.

While the rest of my mind is here, unshaven cheek next to the plastic float. Small rivulets run down the gutters of the float, and I smell the plastic and the smell of the lake water in the sun and a whiff of the sunscreen I slathered on Cal earlier. It all smells like summer.

"Cal, the joke with the fish in the fridge this morning?"
"Yes?"

"It was funny, you two must have planned that carefully. But I had to let them go right away. The fish could have died, and none of us would have wanted that. That would have been sad."

"I'm sorry, Daddy."

"I'm not angry at you. I just want you to be careful with living things. We have to take care of living things that are smaller than us. They deserve to be in the world as much as we do. Understand?"

"Yes."

"Good. Enough on that. Now when we get to the island, we'll go around to where the ladder is, okay?"

"Yep!"

And with that, a thin shroud of doubt that had hung over both of us since the prank this morning was lifted. All was right with the world, and we were here together, and the adventure real. As we neared the float, we talked about what we were doing, what each was doing, and in doing this Cal and I were functioning as a team.

"I'm going to turn the float around, so the other side is against the ladder."

"I'll grab the ladder."

"But don't get up at first."

"I won't get up, but I'll grab the ladder."

"Then get both hands on the ladder to climb it, and slide off the float before you climb the ladder, okay?"

"Okay, but not yet. Almost. Okay, I got it."

"You got it, bud."

I knew this team feeling from other events in life, but I was not sure whether he had known it before. He did it well. It was a fine feeling to share with my son.

He clambered onto the swim dock and I pushed the float up and he pulled it aboard. I climbed up.

"Ah," I said as I sat on the rippled wood.

"Ah," he repeated as he sat.

"We did it."

"Yep!"

"Good job, little bear. You're a good partner."

"You too," he said and clapped me on the shoulder.

37

The late morning gently succumbed to a lazy noon and without any pain afternoon was upon us, still there by the lake. Cal and I had returned from our expedition, after the swim dock had slowly changed from terra incognita to a place we'd been. After we returned, Cal had brought the news of the new land to Sam. They discussed it and other things. I retreated to my chair with the other adults. Some time later, Marissa addressed me.

"Bear, do you know what I'd so love right now?" Marissa says from behind her shades.

"Me?" I answer.

"Yes, particularly if you would get me a cool, hoppy beverage from the cottage. With a lemon wedge, please. I would so love you for that," she smirks.

"Keep an eye on these guys," I say, tilting my head towards Cal and Sam.

"Yep," she says, inattentively. I note that Jeffrey is closest to them, and actually paying attention to them, so I let it go.

If she gets a beer, then I can have a pipe, I think to myself as I walk to the house. I remember right where I left it: on the top of that bi-level table that Neil's parents had donated for the cottage. There in the corner of it was the pencil bag with the pipe in it and the tobacco and the matches.

I make for this as I enter the door. I clean it and pack it and prepare to light it and don't even care that I'm doing it in the cottage. Then in the corner of my eye, I see Jessica coming from the kitchen and she says "I've been thinking that we should just plan the year."

I look up and she is there smiling, in her bathing suit and sarong, going on, "Just sit down the four of us, and I can basically act like everything is going to go on the same forever, like everybody does, and I'll put the calendar on the table and there will be the things we'll do in the fall, and the holiday season, and then maybe a ski trip together in the winter, and into the springtime—maybe Disney—and then we come back around to next summer pretty quickly. All stuff all of us do together, all things Cal and Sam do together. The momentum will help. Don't you think?"

She's a genius. I can't suppress a smirk as I listen to her describe the plan. "You're awesome. Yes. Will Jeffrey be okay with this?"

"He will be. Don't worry about Jeffrey."

"I'm really excited about this. And I'm really happy we both feel the same way."

"We do," she says and without really thinking I open my arms and she hers and we hug. I pull her very tight to me, and I have to suppress the desire to pick her up a little in my giddiness and all the while I try to ignore the feeling of the bare skin of her back under my hands.

Quietly, into her shoulder, I say, "Thank you. Really. Thank you."

I pull away and she smiles beautifully in a way that makes little crinkles around her eyes, and then she kisses me quickly on the cheek. "It's the right thing," she says before she turns and walks out the front screen door towards the sun and the lake and our great shared family. The door cracks shut.

I feel a little shudder of happiness and I pick up my pipe and I light it. Through the screen door I see Jessica's head bob lower and lower towards the beach until she's eclipsed by the frame. After a few puffs I walk to the kitchen.

As I turn the corner, I'm blinded by a hard slap across my face. My pipe flies away and leaves my teeth hurting. It's Marissa, irate. More livid than I've ever seen her. Frightening. She hisses at me:

"You motherFUCKER. How the fuck could you do that?"

"Ww, what?"

She slaps me, hard, again. "I fucking saw you two just now. 'I'm so glad you feel the same way,'" she mimes, acidly.

"No, no, it's not like that at all," I say, realizing how stupid this sounds, how this will only reinforce her suspicion.

"Neil would never, ever . . ." she trails off, shaking her head, shaking. "This is done. This is fucking done. I can't even fucking . . . you stupid, stupid FUCK!" and she punches me, hard, in the stomach and chest.

"No, no!" I say, trying to catch her hands, but she goes on, "That you'd do this to Cal! You're such an asshole! His best friend's fucking MOTHER! Oh god."

She begins to retch. She runs to the bathroom and slams the door. I hear it lock, hear her vomit.

I'm frozen in shock for a moment. My front teeth ache, they feel like they might be loose.

On the cutting board in the kitchen is the lemon. I see it there, the whole lemon I was going to cut into quarters, one of which I was going to place in the mouth of Marissa's beer bottle before I brought it out to her on the beach. None of that will ever happen now.

I can hear Marissa scream in the bathroom. A primal scream. I wonder if the kids can hear that on the beach.

"Marissa!" I shout at the bathroom door. I pound on the door. "Marissa, you're misunderstanding what you heard."

I hear her in a low, feral voice say "No. No. No," before she scream-shouts again. This shout is one word "GO!"

I'm filled with a jittery panic and I need to see Calvert. I need to go pick him up right this second. Whether or not he can hear his mother scream, especially if he can, even if he can't. I fast-walk, nearly a run, out the front door, and break into a run down the lawn. I hear the screen door crack far behind me, it's like someone firing a shot at me, but missing.

As I cross the road to the beach, I hear sounds from the house, it's Marissa, they're odd sounds, but from the volume I realize that her scream probably didn't reach down here. There's Calvert on the beach, just beyond Jessica, still with Sam. The scene is as beautiful as it was ten minutes ago, but curdled now, horrifying. We are in the weightless moment between the ledge and the ground.

Jessica sees my face and her expression changes. As I come closer, she says "What's wrong?"

"Everything. It's all fucked up. Marissa heard us and thinks we're having an affair."

Jessica's expression cycles through shock and then puzzlement then despair.

"She blew up. I think she's going to end it right away."

"Why aren't you up there talking to her? Did you explain?"

"Explain what? No, she's livid."

"You have to talk to her."

"She's throwing up. She's locked in the bathroom. I need Cal."

I go to Cal and pick him up from behind and swing him in a circle with our momentum, then pull him into my arms.

"Daddy!" he says, surprised, vaguely annoyed. His little eyelashes are so long and his cheeks are so round and he has a little food crusted in the corner of his mouth, and he is perfect.

"I love you, little bear," I say. He laughs and I put my face into his neck and make the "rowr rowr rowr" sound and he giggles convulsively. He pushes against my chest to get down and I put him down and he runs back down the beach. I feel like a part of me is being removed, like my insides are being pulled out, streaming down the beach with my little boy.

Jeffrey is reading a book and seems profoundly unaware of anything happening. A powerboat knits a droning seam along the far shore.

Jessica walks up and grips my shoulder and says "Neil, we can explain it to her, she'll . . ."

"What is the explanation, Jessica? What were we talking about? Fooling her out of her plan? Manipulating her? Oh fuck."

"We were talking about something good for Cal. It's about Cal."

"This would take forever to fix. And the time is all gone now. There's no time. Fuck."

Samantha is at Jeffrey's side now, saying something. He is talking back to her, with an eyebrow raised skeptically. "Don't joke about that, honey," he says.

"No, Daddy, really. It's a fire."

I glance up to where Samantha is looking and it's the house. From the right side of the house, from around back it seems, a thin loft of smoke rises. A brief tongue of flame flashes.

The cottage is on fire.

I break into a run. The house bounces in my vision back towards me, but my run feels painfully slow. I can see as I get closer that inside the front door is already hazy.

Inside the door, I can see that the kitchen near the back door is in full flame. The recycling, the pile of newspaper, it must have started from there. I'm surprised at how quiet the fire is. It's not a dramatic roar of flame, it's just a hiss. I pull open the cabinet under the sink and unlatch the fire extinguisher.

"Marissa!" I shout, "Get out of there!"

I pull the pin and aim it at the fire and squeeze the handle and a gust of yellow powder flies out, and stops almost immediately. It has no effect. I shake the extinguisher but it is spent.

"Marissa!" I shout again. "It's a fire! Get out!"

I throw myself against the bathroom door. I briefly see daylight between the frame and the door. I put my shoulder into it again, harder, and it gives way. After the door breaks, I feel a further resistance, and hear a sickening hollow thump. The door jams half open.

I push harder and force my head and one shoulder around the door. Marissa is on the floor, blocking the door. She is moving sluggishly. I realize that the hollow thump must have been her head against the sink. I've probably given her a concussion. Fucking awesome.

"Fuck. Marissa, the house is on fire, we have to get out!" I say, trying to pull her from behind the door into the bathroom. She is disoriented, her eyes are not focusing. Her hands grab at me.

"NO!" She shouts, "Oww, No! You're not!" She shouts. She is not reaching for me to help her, she is pulling me down.

Inside the bathroom is hazy now too, and I feel a catch in my lungs as I try to move her and I begin to cough. I gasp in more haze and cough more. I cannot stop coughing now. There is no clean air. She continues to pull me down, my foot slips and I am on the floor as well. We are jammed in the tiny bathroom, on the floor, coughing, fighting.

On the ceiling, the smoke whorls in blacker streams like ink in water. It's pretty. It will kill us, but it's pretty as it does it. Now we both are coughing, and retching. In between her coughs I think she says "Neil!" I can't see anymore, my eyes are stung and watering and don't want to open anymore.

My lungs are in agony, and my stomach convulses and it feels like we are drowning in a lake of smoke. Each inhalation makes it worse and I want to stop breathing, but my body is not mine anymore and it keeps sucking in the smoke and coughing and convulsing and it goes on and on, and I feel where the panic would be, but it's all eaten up by the pain of the muscles contracting and the cycle of gasping and coughing. It doesn't stop, how will it stop, but now from somewhere creeps into my mind maybe something calmer coming, I think I feel something a little bit better on the other side of the agony, and I feel Marissa's arm between me and the floor and it moves as we both cough and retch and now it all recedes and it's better, it's better.

38

From the shore, the smoke coming from the house climbs and grows like a living thing, from a small gray stream to a black billow. Jessica frantically searches through her bag for her cell phone and is calling 911. The smoke reaches some critical altitude and begins to spread out horizontally, like two great dark flanking wings.

Calvert makes to move towards the house, to cross the street, but Jeffrey puts his hand on his shoulder to stop him. He points back to where Sam clings to Jessica.

"No, Cal," Jeffrey says. "Stay here with your sister."

Acknowledgments

Thanks to Alan Good for taking a risk on this weird little book and for doing all the considerable work of making it physically real in people's hands. Thanks also to my fellow 2022 Malarkists, who will evermore be my graduating classmates.

Roger Vaillancourt is a professional explicator and maker of soothing sounds. He lives in the Boston area.

Other titles from Malarkey Books

The Life of the Party Is Harder to Find Until You're the Last One Around, Adrian Sobol
Forest of Borders, Nicholas Grider
Faith, Itoro Bassey
Music Is Over!, Ben Arzate
Toadstones, Eric Williams
It Came from the Swamp, edited by Joey R. Poole
Deliver Thy Pigs, Joey Hedger
Guess What's Different, Susan Triemert
White People on Vacation, Alex Miller
Man in a Cage, Patrick Nevins
Pontoon, edited by Alan Good
Don Bronco's (Working Title) Shell, Donald Ryan
Fearless, Benjamin Warner
Thunder from a Clear Blue Sky, Justin Bryant
Your Favorite Poet, Leigh Chadwick

malarkeybooks.com